THE WINDSHIP RACE

John Wingate

SAPERE
BOOKS

THE WINDSHIP RACE

Published by Sapere Books.

20 Windermere Drive, Leeds, England, LS17 7UZ,
United Kingdom

saperebooks.com

ISBN:

ACKNOWLEDGEMENTS

Numerous seafarers have contributed in their different ways to the conception and birth of this book. I thank them all, but would especially mention:

Captain Michael M. Willoughby, MRIN, FNI
Colin Mudie, Esq., C.Eng., FRINA, FRIN, MSIAD
Mr John Walker and Mrs Jean Walker of Walker Wingsails
Mr Lloyd Bergeson, Wind Ship Development Corporation, Boston, USA
The Mayor of Boston, Massachusetts, USA
The Harbour Master, Boston, Massachusetts, USA
Mrs Ann Richardson
Doctor R. H. Tuckett of Greytown, North Island, New Zealand
Captain D. W. Galloway, Harbour Master and Chief Pilot (Retired), Wellington Harbour Board, New Zealand
Captain David Kilner
The Royal Institution of Naval Architects, London
The Nautical Institute, London
M. Yves Lemoigne, Docteur ès Sciences, Agrégé d'Université, Université de Lyon
Philip Baker, Esq. DSC, MA
Mrs Kay Forster, secretary and friend for twenty-one years
John Forster, Esq.
Paule, my wife

SHIPS AND THEIR CREWS

MV SHERRILEE USA
Cargo: bulk chemical ores
Aerofoil Wind Ship: 25,300 tons; 163m, 25m, 12m
Twin diesels: service speed, 14kn; 2cp 4-bladed propellers
Sail area, 750m². Max. wind speed for sail use, 70 kn.

Captain: Byrd Klosson
Chief Engineer: Sandy Donaldson
Executive Officer First Mate: Franklin Dicker
Second Mate and Navigating Officer: Jeff Hines
Third Mate: Crane Beverley
Fourth Mate: Peter Tinson
Second, Third and Fourth Engineers
Complement: 28

MV WANDERING STAR Liberia
Cargo: precision engineering parts
Five-masted schooner: 2,412 tons; 69m, 12.2m, 5.9m
Powered sheets

1 *Captain*: George Staithe
2 *Captain*: Roger Buckle
Chief Engineer: Rastus Ahmed
First Mate: Joào Otaz
Second Mate and Navigating Officer: Burn Tinewood
Third Mate: Donald Ferguson
Fourth Mate: Hannah Jones (Assistant Navigating Officer)
Bo'sun: 'Whisky' Zrezczny
Nurse: Jasmine Htut

Chief Stewardess: Doreen Murray
Stewardesses: Rita Carne and Peggy Bishop
Seamen: 12 Nigerians, 8 Lascars, 4 Chinese, 2 Chileans
Engineers: 2 Nigerians, 1 British
Complement: 42

MV RÊVE DE L'AVENIR France

Cargo: Outward — automobile parts; Homeward — uranium ore and general

Container sail catamaran: 124,064 tons; 300m, 60m, 14m

10-masted (Twin 5-aerofoil): maximum sail speed: 24 kn.

4 diesel auxiliary engines, 2 in each float, total HP: 12,000

Captain: Commandant Loic Pennac
First Officer: Emile Crozier
Second Mate: Gerard Leduc
Third Mate: Gaston Fouquier
Complement: 38

MV TECHNO VICTORY Panama

Cargo: Outward — general; Homeward — NZ dairy products

Dynaship: 52,800 tons; 195m, 26m, 11m

Sail area: 33,000m²; Masthead height: 70m

6 rotating masts, 200 ft (65m) ht.

Captain: Roger Buckle
Complement: 36

SV WINDROSE Britain

Cargo: Outward — mixed electronic and engineering; Homeward — mixed double-dumped and wool, and furniture

5-masted barque: 16,800 tons; 140m, 24.6m, 8m

Main engines: two 2,500 bhp diesels, feathering cp. propellers 12kn.

Sail speed: 22kn.

5 hatches; 5 x 25 t cranes

Height of masts: 170 ft (56m)

Captain: Barnaby Jones

First Mate: 1 James Mirson, 2 Karl Karatz, 3 Benjamin Bellew

Second Mate: Benjamin Bellew

Third Mate: Richard Tudgey

Chief Engineer: Hamish Murray

Second Engineer: Peter Solway

Radio Officer: Frank Sisson

Purser: Henry Purl

Bo'sun: 1 Thomas Hawkins, 2 Reginald Posner

Sailmaker: Samuel Tyler (Sails)

Carpenter: Bertrand Hicks (Chippy)

Petty Officers: Ernest Scott and Geoffrey Reddaway

Donkeyman: Frank Stiles

Chief Steward: George Deeds

Cook: Alex Holloway

Assistant Cook: Charles Burn

Starboard Watch: Leading Seaman Tregannon

Port Watch: Leading Seaman Wright

Complement: 57

14 Able Seamen

10 Ordinary Seamen

4 Deck Boys

10 Cadets

PREFACE

I suppose that I knew Jason Mercer better than anyone; and, if the SACOR stakes had not been so colossal, there would also have been no story to tell. The Kremlin's move towards the Gulf started it all, but Gorschkov had to justify his eight million men under arms to his restless people, did he not?

It is old history now, but, after Afghanistan and the demise of the notorious ayatollah, the 'new' Russians trampled across Baluchistan to set up their naval base on the Iran frontier. Gwatar had the advantage of an existing airfield; from Point Fastah, the Gulf of Oman fell immediately under the control of the Red Fleet.

Within weeks of this invasion, the world was once again talking of fossil fuels becoming extinct. The actual spot bunker price Rotterdam fuel oil (1500 secs) was within sight of one hundred dollars a barrel, and no one could forecast a levelling-off. The result was a rocketing of the dollar, until heavy fuels for the diesel ships of the West became so costly that the majority of shipowners were compelled to put their money where they professed their hearts were. But a minority had such enormous capital investment locked up in their motor ships that to switch to 'sail-assisted' would have been a crippling blow … so the supranational consortium was created to organize SACOR, the Sail-Assisted Commercial Ocean Race.

Three years' advance notice had been given. On 21 January, the Outward Race had started from South Foreland to New Zealand. The 'Outward' Winner was *Techno Victory*; the Winner-on-Time, *Wandering Star*, the result being a sobering shock to *Windrose* and many of the others. But, because the Overall Winner was to be the ship whose combined results of the 'Outward' *and* 'Homeward' made the greatest profit for her owner, there was still hope for those other twenty-four ships gathered for the start in Wellington on Sunday, 23 July for the Homeward Race.

If you asked Jason who was his best 'mucker', I think I could claim the privilege. I hope so, because he was one of the most interesting seafarers I have run up against, both notorious and famous. We were together at the Warsash Navigation School.

He was the outstanding athlete of our reasonably successful bunch, and we used to chiakk him about his unconventional habits. He drank little, preferring to spend his pay on canoeing, long-distance running and karate. His delight was scaling mountains, which is why my parents, who live in Snowdonia, always had their house open for him. He was a quiet man, well over six feet, I reckon; he was an extrovert with a sense of fun, but dependable. When he lost interest in someone, you knew that you too could write them off.

It was at Warsash too that I met Hannah Jones, a few years after we'd been to sea. Whereas Mercer was fair-haired with the distant, blue eyes of the dreamer, she was petite, dark and mysterious: an Irish colleen, I first judged her. Her father, Captain Barnaby Jones, Extra Master Mariner, was a formidable sea captain. He still wore his faded Falkland medals and was one of the old school who knew what he wanted from his company and got it. He and Gavin McBinney were Joint Managing Directors of the Ocean Navigating Company which owned *Windrose*, but they were struggling against the monopoly of the Big Boys when the second oil crisis blew up. They decided to place *all* their eggs in the SACOR basket, particularly as Barnaby Jones was an outstanding seaman. He was happier commanding a ship than pushing bumph around in the offices of the Ocean Navigating Company, the shares of which were crumbling daily.

I am compelled to mention Stok, the unforgettable Akroyd Stok. I was unlucky enough to meet him at interview when I signed on as Second Mate of *Techno Power*, one of the early ships in his container fleet. Of the few loathsome characters I have bumped up against, Akroyd Stok still heads the list. Powerful and ruthless in his supranational dealings, he stopped at nothing to achieve his ends. I should know — and so should those others who over the years have blundered across his path. With hit squads moving with impunity around the world, even those who are still living will hesitate, I know, to emerge from their holes to back me up. But I am determined to tell this story, if only for the true record. Anonymity being therefore my only sure shield, I present this narrative under the name by which Jason Mercer knew me best: R.O. *'Mucker'*.

SACOR CONCEPT AND RULES

Following the overnight, severe increases in the oil price

When SACOR (Sail-Assisted Commercial Ocean Race) was originally proposed to the International Shipping Owners' Committee, it was unanimously agreed that one criterion only pertained: *the sail-assisted ship who made the most profit for her owner would be the overall winner.*

Rules can be designed either to achieve fairness, or to guide events towards the direction in which the Owners wish them to go. Profit is all that matters to the Consortium: the Race Rules have therefore been designed to that end. When operating a merchant ship, *the following factors will affect the profit which she makes for her Owner:*

A. No Owner will add a sail-assist component to his vessel merely to save fuel. In the eighties, the public could not understand why Owners did not build sail-assisted ships: there were many vessels laid up round the world which could have been bought for knock-down prices in order to have sails fitted.

B. The welfare of the snowy owl does not concern shipowners. Ecology plays no part in an Owner's decision. It is not because the planet's oil is being gobbled up that Owners decide to go 'sail-assisted'. It is because of the astronomical price of Actual Spot Bunker Price Rotterdam Fuel Oil (1500 secs) at 107 dollars/barrel: (the period which this book describes) nearly six times the price it was when the oil crisis broke in 1973.

It therefore pays Owners to invest capital in newly designed, sail-assisted ships, even when the price of coal and coal-derived oils is cheaper than oil.

C. The cost of the ship: a vessel has a life of between twenty and twenty-five years. A tanker has to make enough profit for herself within two all-round voyages. A more expensive ship will take longer to recoup her building costs. She must stay at sea for twenty years, whereas in contrast, an ocean-racer is scrapped after one trip. The cost of the ship and how long she can profitably work are therefore important factors to consider when rating her for SACOR. The Baltic Exchange, Britain's ship-broking authority, will assess the capital cost of each competitor and her running costs. Insurance represents a large slice of a ship's costs: Lloyds will assess each vessel's insurance premium and will decide the replacement value of each ship.

D. A selected classification society will provide a coefficient 'factor' for the lifespan of each vessel, this factor being set against the capital cost of each ship, e.g.: if a ship, A, has a life of two years, and, B, a life of twenty, ship A has a coefficient factor of 10 against her life, relative to ship B. This coefficient will be included when calculating the ship's rating.

E. Owners consider crew's wages as 'Crew Profit': each crewman makes a 'profit' when he sells his service. When he goes ashore, he walks down the gangway with that 'profit' in his pocket.

F. There are no rulings regarding union labour: each ship will make her own arrangements and take the consequences.

G. The value of the cargo multiplied by the number of days it is out of circulation represents the cost of the cargo. The interest which is lost on this dormant money represents a heavy cost in the final analysis. A rowing-boat with a cargo of pearls; or the QE 11 with a load of hay? Neither are likely to win SACOR.

H. The day-to-day running costs will be added: stores, spares, crew requirements, annual refit, scrubbing, docking costs, depreciation and, most importantly, the cost of fuel.

J. Each competitor must be fitted with auxiliary mechanical power for manoeuvring and safety purposes: it is up to the designer and Owner to decide what engine will provide most profit at the end of the race. If too big an engine is installed and too much fuel is bunkered, unnecessary capital is tied up and is out of circulation.

K. The speeds of turn-round and cargo-handling affect costs. Loading and unloading machinery affects the design of the ship; profit cannot be assessed until it is known how long it takes to load and discharge cargo. If *any* cargo were allowed to be carried, a realistic rating would be impossible. Each competitor will therefore be required to carry a standard cargo and this provision will thereby provide a 'constant' for each ship.

L. The most difficult problem in designing and calculating the rating formula has been how to rate the cargo.

Costs of shipping cargo from Wellington to South Foreland and to British and European ports are the Owners' CREDITS and these are known as 'returns'.

The value of 'returns' minus 'costs' represents the Owners' profit.

Homeward

1. Ships bound through the Panama Canal are to call at Colón and Kingston, Jamaica. Ships making The Horn passage are to call at Montevideo and Rio de Janeiro. The starts from these ports will be decided at the time.

2. All ships will then proceed to Belém, Brazil, where they will remain for one week after the last ship has arrived. The start from Belém for the Boston leg will be controlled and in reverse order.

3. It is realized that the Panama ships will gain 209 miles. But to offset their advantage over the Horn ships, it should be remembered that the Panama contingent will have headwinds in the Caribbean during July, and that the Caribbean and Northern Brazilian currents are adverse. The Rio ships will have the Brazil current against them until Cabo do Calcanhar but, once the Cape is turned, they will benefit from the South Equatorial current which will be against the Panama ships.

4. Each ship will carry a Race Observer who will be competent in the English language or in that of the ship's nationality.

5. Race Observers will exchange ships at the four ports of call. The Panama ships: at Balboa, Kingston, Belém and Boston. The Horn ships: at Montevideo, Rio de Janeiro, Belém and Boston. Exchange of ROS will not be announced until the day before sailing at each obligatory port of call.

6. All competitors will be rated both for the Outward and Homeward legs; the sum of both legs will decide the winner.

7. Each ship will load fifteen forty-foot container dry vans: normal weight of box 3.8 tons; all-up weight of each box to be above twenty tons. Maximum all-up weight, 304 tons. A minimum of dry vans is to be stowed on deck; a minimum of fifteen dry vans to be carried. When the last slings are slipped on the quayside during the final unloading, the race is deemed to be ended for the competitor. Passenger ships excluded.

8. The method by which the Rating Committee calculates its formula will remain secret. Ships' ratings will be published before the Outward and Homeward starts.

9. The SACOR computer is in SACOR House, the Barbican, London. The Baltic Exchange and Lloyds will jointly monitor the operation of the computer.

10. There will be no appeal against natural or man-inspired disasters.

11. The prize of fifty million dollars will be paid to the overall winner on the day on which the results are announced.

CHAPTER ONE: ROUGH PERSUASION

'Is that Mr Mercer?'

'Ye-e-s?'

'Jason Mercer?'

'Yes. Who's that speaking?' the Race Observer retorted through the telephone at the head of the gangway which was creaking to-and-fro upon MV *Sherrilee*'s upper deck. Mercer was suspicious; he'd heard that aged corn-crake voice before: very English, authoritative…

'I've been trying to trace you. Captain Jones here. You're in *Sherrilee* at Waterloo Quay Wharf, aren't you?'

'Yes, sir.' He'd been Barnaby Jones's Fourth Mate way back, an unforgettable apprenticeship. 'Old Barnacle' sounded tense, uptight: unusual for the old dragon…

'*Windrose* is at anchor in her starting berth, but there's a service boat in ten minutes. Meet me for dinner: the Coromandel in half an hour.' There could be no excuse. It was an order.

'Thanks, sir. I'll be…' The line clicked.

Jason James Mercer pursed his lips. Old Barnacle had not mellowed with the years. The Coromandel was near the Parliament Building, and Jason knew it from the old days: he had been serving in one of Cunard's ACT ships, on the refrigerated run between Southampton, Charleston and Wellington, before Southampton had committed suicide.

He went below to the cabin, which was his for this first leg of the Homeward race. Whether the first port of call was to be Montevideo or Balboa depended upon Captain Byrd Klosson's announcement tomorrow before the start. The odds-on in the bars was for Panama, because a wind sail ship profited not at all from the westerly winds which The Horn passage ordained. It was rumoured that the owners of the 25,300-ton *Sherrilee* was the same company which, under a different name, also owned the similar wind sail, the Japanese registered *Siddartho Maru* of 31,600 tons; if true, it was certain that each would take the alternative route for comparison between the two passages … and, slipping from his reefer, Jason began cleaning up for dinner.

The half-scraped face squinting back at him from the mirror looked drawn for his twenty-seven years. The imprint of this last year without a ship was starting to show in the taut, half-moon lines at the corners of his wide mouth. But, though he was relieved to note that a sense of fun still lurked in his eyes, flecks of grey were already showing among the fair hair of his temples. He was an inch over six feet and was sturdily built. But his arms had always seemed to him out of proportion to the rest of his body: they were too long, his large hands protruding like hams from his sleeves. He could still remember his adolescence and the embarrassment of not knowing how to hide these hands… The ship's water was soft from the distillers, and he rinsed the soapy film from his cheeks before fumbling for the aftershave.

Tonight, Saturday, 22 June, could be the last decent meal between here and the other side of South America. Secretly he preferred the Panama route, but there was kudos via The Horn. At this time of the year, even ships as large as *Sherrilee* would move about a bit, if legend was accurate: his father, in contented retirement with his mother at Winchester, had been round The Horn on one of the first world yacht races. He never let his son hear the end of it. Jason smiled to himself: it was Dad who had pushed him to sea…

Jason got this job as Race Observer at the last moment (his aircraft had landed in Wellington only two days ago) because of sickness on the ROS' establishment. He had applied for the *Windrose* vacancy as First Mate but James Mirson, ex-Pangbourne Nautical School, had pipped him at the post.

Mirson had been at Warsash too; they'd known each other and had become friends, the continuous muddle over names bringing them together; it was a good solid friendship, and they had kept in touch. *A pity*, thought Jason, *we've not been able to meet here: Jamie must be up to his eyeballs with work — and with Barnaby Jones watching over him!* The ship was victualling for a trip which would mean survival or oblivion for McBinney and Jones; the Ocean Navigating Company was a small shipping line. And as Jason Mercer brushed down his unruly fair hair, sleeking the longer bits behind his ears, he remembered the rumours rampant in the port. If he had the nerve, he'd ask Old Barnacle how much truth there was in the buzz…

A shadowy sixty-year-old tycoon named Akroyd Stok was apparently behind the whole SACOR idea; he ran an international empire with tentacles rippling in every corner of the globe. Jason had met Stok briefly at SACOR headquarters during that last-minute interview for the job of Race Observer. Stok exuded an overpowering presence, an indefinable aura in the room. Jason was reminded of a cobra he had watched in Bombay, its evil head weaving gently back and forth, its scaly lids hooded over jet-black, shining eyes. 'Lethally ruthless,' they said: an understatement if ever there was one. The man, in Jason's judgement, would slit a baby's throat if it paid him … and even here, as Jason left the solitude of his minute cabin, he sensed again the revulsion he had felt. Dammit, Akroyd Stok's supranational company, Global Sea Transport (GST), was bigger than even the giant consortiums like P&O and the

Australian National Line (ANL). Stok owned, in one way or another, four ships among the competitors.

It was this monopolistic pressure which was hotting up the temperature and creating bad feelings: gossip along the waterfront was that Stok's *Techno Victory*, GST's huge dynaship of 52,800 tons, was entered to make certain that *Windrose*, McBinney and Jones's classical five-masted barque, was soundly thrashed. Not only was the hundred-million-dollar prize worth the gaining, but the winner would undoubtedly become the prototype for the world's future non-nuclear ships. Jason checked the money in his wallet, put on his anorak and left his cabin.

It was whispered, too, that should Stok win, this would be the death knell for sail-assisted ships for years to come. Stok's multinationals had already snatched and bought up the wool wharfage in Australia, and had manipulated the unions to 'black' *Windrose* and others who might try to emulate her. *Windrose* was too profitable and a threat to the freight carried by Global Sea Transport. *Yes*, thought Jason, as he stepped out into the glaring lights of *Sherrilee*'s upper deck, *there'll be trouble on this race homewards, if the tension remains as high as it is.* At the ROS' last meeting yesterday in the Harbour Master's office, the Senior RO had been forced to ask them all to do what they could to reduce the bad feeling. Jason shrugged his shoulders as he pattered down the gangway: *he* could do little about it. What surprised him was how Stok had managed to retain so much influence in SACOR ... and for a moment Jason paused on the quay to glance up at the stark, functional ship towering above him.

Sherrilee was a general cargo vessel, 163 metres long. The Stars and Stripes flapped at the main mast tucked into the after end of her bridge. Her lines were functionally powerful, like so many modern ships with their square sterns, but what made her so grotesque were the two 180-feet-high multiple aerofoil sails at each end. The twin, five-vaned multiple aerofoils were looming just clear of the bridge and above the truck of the foremast. They whispered high above him in the night, the lights from the city reflecting eerily upon the 'sails' idling to the strong breeze. Jason wondered what she would be like at sea with that frightening top-hamper. But Wind Sails knew what they were at. Under the command of Byrd Klosson, she seemed to be a happy ship. Her 'Exec.', as the Mate was known on board this American ship, was Franklin Dicker, a smiling, open-hearted Texan whom Jason liked immediately. Klosson, a mid-Westerner, was more aloof and had the reputation of being anti-'Limey'. *Well, I'll soon know*, Jason thought as he lengthened his stride towards the Queen's Wharf.

The service boat was already bobbing alongside the pontoon at the Service Jetty, for she had completed her rounds of the ships already anchored out on the starting line. *Sherrilee* would be slipping at 2300 tonight, Klosson having decided to give his crew one more run ashore. But Captain Jones had refused leave tonight: a prudent decision, but one which reemphasized his reputation for being a hard skipper. Unlike many other ships, his company would not have thick heads for the start tomorrow, Sunday, 23 June, at 1100. Feeling like a sprog cadet, Mercer hurried out of the docks towards the city and the Parliament Building.

Barnaby Jones was looking at his wristwatch when Jason entered the dimly lit bar. Thickset and robust, in his reefer and brass buttons there was no mistaking his profession. Tufts of grey fuzz sprouted from his eyebrows and ears; his skin was leathery and lined. His wide mouth was thin-lipped, like a rat-trap. Hard duty had left its stamp on this mariner's face, thought Jason, who had served him as a boy in *Hilda Jones*, the four-masted barque which was Old Barnacle's first command.

'Beer?'

'Thanks. Sorry I'm a bit late.'

'Take our drinks in, shall we?'

Following the master mariner, Jason was surprised to note how powerfully built Jones was: stocky, tough, there was not a bit of flab on him. The only sign of ageing (he must have been in his early fifties) were the creases at the rear of his neck and the freckles on the backs of his hands.

'Here, in the corner. I want to talk.'

He ordered the cheaper of the two menus and another pint of bitter. When the waitress, a fair-haired girl with an accent like honey, minced off to the kitchen, Captain Jones came straight to the issue.

'Glad you came, Mercer. Bit of an emergency and I want your help.' He fished out a gnarled black pipe from his pocket; he looked longingly at it, glanced round the room, then re-stowed it.

'Yes, if I can be of any use.'

'We've bumped into each other socially, haven't we? You've met my Hannah? In *Hilda Jones*?'

'No, at the Nav. School. Your daughter took me to your home once in Locks Heath, but you'd gone out.'

Hannah Jones was a good-looker and they had kept in touch on a Christmas card basis. Their last meeting had been at the Squawking Parrot at Bursledon; it was she who had pointed out the ad in *Sailing Monthly*. She had already signed on as Navigator's Assistant in *Wandering Star*, the five-masted schooner operating under the Liberian flag. It had been good to see her yesterday at the SACOR final meeting; someone from home. How could such a hard man as Jones have fathered such a gorgeous girl?

'You listening, Mercer?'

'Yes.'

'I'm asking whether you know my First Mate, James Mirson? He knows you: even looks like you a bit.'

Jason took a gulp of his beer: 'We were cadets together.'

Barnaby Jones leaned on the table and was about to speak when the head waiter coasted towards them.

'Captain Jones, there's a message for you. Just been dropped in by a lady. "I can't wait," she said.' The buff envelope was addressed to Captain Jones in an educated hand.

The Captain waited for the man to withdraw, then peered slowly around the room, before slitting open the envelope. He glanced at the note, then handed it across to Jason. 'The fifth we've had altogether,' was all he said.

'*We told you what you have to do. And we told you not to squeal.*' The message was in red printed capitals. There was no signature.

Jason looked up and into the ageing Captain's angry, blue eyes. Jones began to talk. He spoke rapidly in a low monotone, with his gaze casting around the room continually and watching the door. The soup grew cold while he swung into his stride.

'Better get on with your soup,' the Captain said. He slurped the stuff down, then finished his tale. 'There you are. That's why I've wanted to see you.'

'What can I do?' Jason complained. 'I'm not even in the same ship as James Mirson. I'm an RO, not a ship's officer.'

James Mirson had himself received three mysterious messages, all threats against his own life. The first at Felixstowe before sailing, the others here in Wellington, and all in the same handwriting. Each warned Mirson to leave *Windrose*, if he wanted to remain alive.

'What are they playing at and who are *they*?' Jason asked.

Jones lowered his voice to a whisper: 'You know that Mirson is an exceptional Mate and a hard driver. My Second's too weak. *They* know that *Windrose* will make her best passage with Mirson and I working together. Finally, last night and after the latest warning, James told me he was losing his nerve. He's got a fine wife and they have three children. He's suggested *you* should relieve him while he slips up to Auckland for a plane home.' Those deep blue eyes were staring through Jason. '"*They*" is Stok's mafia.'

'Me? But...'

Jones interrupted: 'You'll soon pick it up again, Mr Mercer.' There was a flicker of amusement in the brittle, watching eyes. 'I seem to remember you used to be one of the fastest boys aloft when furling the royals.'

Jason shook his head. 'We're sailing in twelve hours. Be reasonable, Captain Jones.'

'I need you. *Windrose* needs you, damn you, boy!'

'I'm under contract to SACOR,' Jason emphasized heatedly. 'Stop trying to bully me. I couldn't come, even if I wanted.' He looked across at this man who never would take 'no'. There was disappointment there now, in that hard look. Fortunately, they had finished the coffee. Jason pushed back his chair.

'Thanks,' he said quietly. 'But I can't break a contract, however much pressure you put on the Senior Race Observer. Blair Hamilton can't do anything at this stage, but, anyway, you'll be seeing him later at the principal reporting ports, Belém and Boston.'

The man seemed to crumple. 'All right, Mercer. I'll cope. Perhaps Mr Mirson will have more spunk in him tomorrow morning.' He jerked up his head.

'What time's *Sherrilee* sailing?'

'Twenty-three hundred.'

'Ten minutes to my last boat. Come with me, then.'

He paid up and together they walked back to the docks. The wind was blowing, icy rain slicing horizontally across the pavement. They tried to keep close to the buildings, while traffic swished past on the gleaming wet roads. A taxi swept by and they saw it drawing up at the Service Jetty.

'Bloody, ain't it?' Jones was talking to himself as he crossed the road to the harbour side. Jason kept to windward of him as they both drew their anorak hoods over their heads. When they were only a hundred and fifty yards from the jetty, Jason heard footsteps splashing behind him. He jerked round. Three men, grotesque in their stockinged faces, were charging straight at them. They were flicking short iron bars in their raised hands.

'Look out!' Jason yelled.

Dodging sideways, he tripped the first lout, who slithered into the gutter. Barnaby stood squarely while Jason with a karate chop spiralled the second straight over the quayside and into the black water. They heard him threshing frenziedly while the third hitman took to his heels.

'*All right?*' But even as Jason gasped the question, he heard the swishing of a fast-approaching car. Its headlights were dazzling as it steered straight for them. The engine whined suddenly. At the last instant, with its square Mercedes bonnet gleaming in front of them, Barnaby jabbed hard at Jason. Both fell backwards behind a massive bollard. Tyres squealed; wheels hissed through pools of water. The Mercedes turned in its length, backed, then leaped forward to disappear down a dockland road.

'See what I mean, Mercer?' Captain Jones was picking himself out of the mire. 'Sporting rivals we have, don't we?' He hurried on down to the jetty where the packed boat was bobbing alongside the pontoon and preparing to cast off. He looked up and waved. The last glimpse which Jason had of Old Barnacle was of him wringing water from the tail of his reefer.

The trembling of Jason's limbs had only just ceased when he reached *Sherrilee*. The gangway was lifted behind him as the cable party began singling-up. Captain Klosson stared critically but said nothing when Jason took his place in the port side of the wheelhouse. A pool of water began to form on the vinyl flooring at Jason's feet.

'All ready on the fo'c'sle, Cap'n,' Exec. Dicker reported from his phone. It was interesting for Jason to watch how the Americans ran this merchant ship, navy-wise, like the Russians.

Klosson was looking at him. 'Run into trouble, Mr Mercer?'

'Just a bit, Captain. I'd like to get through to the police, if the port wave's not too busy.'

'Sure? That bad, is it?' The Captain returned to the business of leaving harbour: 'Let go bow rope…'

The headrope splashed invisibly into the black water. The after deck phone was buzzing. Exec. Dicker glanced at the seaman whose face looked like a pale, round melon.

The man covered the mouthpiece with his hand: 'They've found a dead man, sir. Caught on the fender.'

'Say again!' Klosson shouted, unbelieving.

'Corpse, Cap'n. Between the piles and the fender.' The young seaman was going to be sick.

'They're hauling him … *it* in, sir.'

'Send the bow rope out again, Exec.,' the Captain ordered resignedly. 'Guess we'll be here for quite a time.'

Jason heard the footsteps clambering up the steel ladder; a seaman stood at the door to the wheelhouse. 'We found this tied to him, Captain. Round the neck, it was…'

The sodden board was smeared with red capital letters: *MIRSON REFUSED TO LISTEN.*

Jason silently left the bridge. He owed it to his friend, he knew, to identify him. But his heart was hammering and he felt nauseated.

CHAPTER TWO: THE START

Sunday, 23 June

'Aft all main sheets,' Captain Staithe commanded through the mic of *Wandering Star*'s broadcast system. 'Weigh, full speed.'

Hannah Jones stood with Burn Tinewood at the chart table tucked into the port corner of the great schooner's wheelhouse. The navigator was sprawled across the chart, dividers pricking off distances from Pencarrow Head. Yesterday she had laid off the Great Circle passages on the gnomonic chart, one to Panama, the other to The Horn: Extra Master Mariner George Staithe had kept his route intentions to himself. Once outside The Heads, he would be announcing his decision and, *Wandering Star* being fore-and-aft rig, all the betting was on Panama. In her heart, Hannah longed for it to be so. The Horn, for her, was something she preferred not to think about.

The duel was to be between them and their fore-and-aft rival, the big Yank, the 8,014-ton *Sea Falcon*. She had already plumped publicly for Panama, a decision which posed a guessing game for the *Star*'s navigators. And Hannah, having nothing to do at this moment (Burn Tinewood had made it plain that he was to pilot the ship clear of The Heads before she would be trusted to take over), moved towards the starboard wing. She might catch sight of Jason Mercer if *Sherrilee* came within reasonable distance. But his big American Wind Ship would probably take the other route, and then Belém in North Brazil would be their next common port of call. She slid back the wheelhouse door and was met by the pandemonium of thundering canvas, a bedlam which subsided as the powered mainsheets hauled in the booms. The foresails were bent on but still stopped down, ready for instant hoisting once the ship could clear Point Halswell.

Hannah watched the cable party wrestling with the jerking cable when the ship leaned to the wind; then silently, powerfully, *Wandering Star* gathered way. In less than a minute she was gliding through the water, her mainsails sheeted-in, bar taut. As the *Star* settled hard on the wind, her bows were pointing straight for Eastbourne on the far side of the port. What an amazing sight it was, this fleet of ships bustling across the vast harbour flecked by breaking seas! On either side of *Wandering Star*, twenty-three other ships were straining to close Point Halswell, so that they could round up before Ward Island, the rock three-quarters of a mile west of Eastbourne.

Point Jerningham, swarming with spectators, was already abaft the beam as the *Star* leapt ahead of the others across Evans Bay. To windward of her and nearest to land was the impressive *Techno Victory*, their 'chummy ship'. Her white, rigid sails on their identical six masts made an amazing sight as she listed to the fresh breeze. All the sails on each mast were slanted at the same angle to the wind and she seemed to be flying across the surface, her orange hull, light-blue upperworks and violet bulwarks gleaming in the sunlight. She was a giant, compared with the other dynaships: the German, *Pollux*, and the awesome Belgian, the 27,200-ton *Dynasaur*, with her two three-hundred-foot masts. She was only half *Techno Victory*'s displacement, yet she carried two-thirds the sail area of that of the Stok ship. Hannah hurried round the after end of the bridge to see how the start was progressing to leeward.

Most of the fleet were to leeward of the *Star*: Hannah counted eighteen hulls thrashing eastwards towards Point

Halswell. Some of them, notably the Saudi giant, *Hijaz*, of 211,000 tons, seemed to be stopped. She and several others, the Singaporean, *Ocean Kite*, and the Soviet's Costa Rican, *Red Star*, were hove-to: they must be waiting for the hurly-burly to subside before committing themselves to the channel and The Heads. And then Hannah's heart lifted when she saw her father's beautiful ship: *Windrose*, with her sails still furled, was butting up into the wind which was now steady from the south-east. He was plugging her out under power, prudent old seaman that he was: she could see the black dots of men still working on the fo'c'sle, as she had seen them so often, securing for sea. With The Horn ahead of them, this evolution was vital to the ship and she felt relieved that her dad had signed on that driver, James Mirson, for his Mate. With Bo'sun Tom Hawkins lashing the anchor and cables, *Windrose* was in as good hands as her father could wish for. The barque was making up steadily to windward, but was well astern of *Techno Victory* and the others who were jostling for a clear lead at the start.

The Frenchman, the visionary ten-masted catamaran *Rêve de l'Avenir*, was an incredible sight, her twin batteries of extendible aerofoils angled parallel to each other as she fought up to windward. She looked smaller than she really was, for she displaced 124,064 tons. Spray was drifting high from her knife-like 'cat' bows, and Hannah could just make out the rows of container boxes stowed in the cavernous well abaft the fore aerofoil deck. Her 'spacecraft' bridge was perched centrally on this deck, at the feet of the central 'sails' and high above the sea threshing between the two lean hulls. She was not flying the 'motoring' flag, so presumably was under sail only: she must be doing all of twenty knots, thought Hannah, and was a breath-taking sight with that spume flying forty feet into the air. And while the cat flew ahead, Hannah saw *Sherrilee* appearing from behind the Frenchman's sails and steering straight towards *Wandering Star*.

To the eastward of Jason Mercer's ship was her rival, the Japanese *Siddartho Maru*, the other 'wing sail' who was competing with *Sherrilee* for the best route. Perhaps, Hannah thought, she might spot Jason if *Sherrilee* kept on coming this way; he *might* be on the bridge and looking out for her. All at once, Hannah felt she wanted to see someone she knew, and Jason preferably. And as she waited for the steady bearing to bring the two ships closer, she watched the leaders, those strange ships with their high towers, the Flettner rotor ships, battling it out ahead with the extraordinary windmill ships.

Already the windmills were two miles ahead, the seas lolloping against their bluff bows while they steamed contemptuously into the eyes of the wind. *Techno Phanta* was there, her three huge propellers flailing above her in terrifying circles; just astern was *Stella Venus*, the Italian ducted-fan and kite ship who had already declared for The Horn. A couple of cables astern of them, and threshing southwards, was the advanced Flettner, the Dutch *Mina*. The Portuguese vertical turbine ship, *Sao Isabel*, was in the lead and forging ahead rapidly with her double-hoops, each one hundred and fifty feet high, murderously revolving around her two spikey masts. When *Sao Isabel* began to swing off to port, Hannah realized that Captain Staithe, having scythed to the van of the fleet, was taking *Wandering Star* about, and, still without engine, was beating out through the channel. Hannah watched the foresails gliding up their stays, then suddenly filling with astonishing precision, the result of Staithe's driving and drilling. And as the foresails were being sheeted home, the great schooner seemed to leap forward under her most advantageous point of sailing.

The spray was flying across her bows to reach as far aft as the mizzen mast. She must be making over twenty knots through the water, Hannah estimated.

The windmills and the Flettners were growing larger and Hannah sensed, despite her distrust of Staithe, a jolt of pride in being part of this superb schooner. Pride, but resentment too, for she had just discovered that this was a GST ship built expressly to put her father out of business, a disaster which she knew would kill his spirit. Of course, they had never hinted this at interview: she felt tricked, cheated.

Beacon Hill Signal Station was coming abeam, high above them in Strathmore Park; and as Point Dorset fell astern on their starboard quarter, Hannah could at last pick out the white seas breaking upon Barrett Reef. The channel between Palmer Head and the reef seemed crowded enough already, the leading ships bunching as they fought for precedence: the Flettners and windmills were now at least two miles ahead, although the *Star* and the American, *Sea Falcon*, who was overhauling from astern, were rapidly gaining on the leaders. The open sea was visible ahead, a strip of confused water jerking on the horizon, with nothing between *Wandering Star* and the ice of the Antarctic. Hannah turned to watch the remainder of the field, which was beginning to round Point Dorset.

The big ships, *Hijaz, Red Star* and *Ocean Kite* were well astern, calmly accepting that, for them, there could be no unseemly barging match as they entered the restricted entrance to the port. *Hijaz* was taking the lead, while the other monsters were falling in astern of her. The red and white flags were flying from their masts, and presumably the pilots would be taken off by helicopter or pilot tugs once the ships were outside. Ahead of these giants, the smaller barques and dynaships were jostling for position but, try as Hannah might, she could not sight the 'honorary' entrant: presumably the *Ark's* low freeboard and greenhouse upperworks were already below the horizon. *Planet Earth*, that colossal raft entered by the UN, was being allowed to join the party in the Caribbean.

Hannah felt uneasy about the bunching off Point Dorset, as she counted the hulls now lining up for the tricky passage. There was the Spanish passenger cruise clipper, the 7,400-ton *Reina de la Mar* designed by Colin Mudie, the elegance of her pale-blue hull and white upperworks being, Hannah thought, marred by the red and yellow band of her rails. She wondered what the four hundred passengers must be feeling as, at last, they must be realizing what they were in for. The company had pitched for the Panama route: apparently lots had to be drawn for the berths, such was the popularity of the project. A beauty, she looked, the other aristocrat among these ugly, functional ships bunching for precedence as they started to negotiate Barrett Reef.

All the big 'sailers' were jumbled together. She could picture her father fuming on *Windrose*'s bridge; he could never accept this new ruthlessness at sea. 'Courtesy of the sea': the maxim by which he steered his nautical career had become hollow tradition, nothing else. But *what*, for goodness sake, was *Techno Victory* doing?

CHAPTER THREE: BAD JOSS

Captain Jones glanced up at the yards: the hands had been aloft too long already. It was cold, but his men had spent enough time in *Windrose* to know that whatever he ordered was for the benefit of the ship. They'd be sucking their teeth, but as soon as the ship was clear of the channel, he would get them down from aloft. It was prudent, with this continuing hurly-burly, to keep both watches on deck: not only were they keen to see what was going on but, with so many idiots about, anything could happen.

'Watch your course, Mr Bellew. Nothing to port.'

'Aye, aye, sir; nothing to port.'

The Second, Benjamin Bellew, was now promoted to First Mate since Mirson's murder yesterday, though he was a feeble shadow of his predecessor: pleasant enough, but he was a 'popularity Jack' with the crew and would need watching; and Captain Jones felt as if a ton weight had been dumped on his shoulders since the awful killing of James Mirson last night. *The Horn passage*, Jones thought, *will be exhausting enough without my having to supervise Bellew. It will be tricky supporting him when he makes stupid decisions.* The Bo'sun and Sailmaker were old hands and Boatswain Tom Hawkins had a way of showing his contempt.

'*Nothing* to port, I said.' Captain Jones was already irritated by Bellew. Couldn't the fellow even oversee the quartermaster steering a course? And Barnaby Jones moved across to starboard to see ahead better. The Chief was there, the wind blowing through his silvery hair: he was lucky and could trust his 'Second', the Second Engineer.

'Just as well I've got your diesel engines, Chief,' Jones muttered. 'I wouldn't have liked this lot under sail only.'

The soft accents of the Scot from Peterhead were barely audible in the buffeting of the wind: 'You won't be wanting them once we get clear…' Chief Engineer Hamish Murray showed his broken teeth in a rare smile. 'You'll have enough of this stuff…' He nodded towards the heavens. 'All the way to Montevideo, she'll be making more than her twelve, I'll warrant.'

'Even laden as we are and reefed down, she'll make good fifteen in this wind, Chief. Twenty-two on passage up to Montevideo, perhaps.' *Windrose*'s holds were bursting with wool, her container boxes jammed full of furniture.

'It's as well we had the bad weather comin' out, sir: shaken the lads into shape.'

Jones nodded — this was true, especially now without Mirson. His driving and the weeks of sail-handling on the way out had trained the green hands (and that was sixty per cent of the crew) better than months of theory ashore. Barnaby knew he had James to thank for that. They had feared Mirson but respected him, knowing that their captain would apply the discipline they had agreed to when signing on.

Most of *Windrose*'s hands were disenchanted with the union. They preferred their competency to be judged for what it was worth, which was why they had all signed to Captain Jones's equivalence of naval discipline. Under Bo'sun Hawkins, they were virtually organizing themselves and a skulker got short shrift. But the Bo'sun's promotion meant that Hawkins could not be chasing the crew and also be keeping a bridge watch. Stott, the Senior Petty Officer, had stepped up into Hawkins's shoes, but was not of the same calibre. He was loud-mouthed and already they were calling him the 'Mini-Bo'. Captain Jones turned his attention towards the shipping bearing down on *Windrose* from the other side. He must conceal his anxieties even from the Chief. Perhaps Gavin McBinney could fly out a relief First Mate to Montevideo?

When the Chief went below, Captain Jones focused his binoculars on *Techno Victory*, the big dynaship closing on *Windrose*'s starboard bow.

Although he knew little of her Captain, Randy Buckle, and disliked all that Global Sea Transport stood for, Jones had to admit that the dynaship was a fine sight. She looked like a huge plastic toy, with her six masts, each 73 metres high and carrying her rigid 'sails' which turned with their masts; to furl, her sails were drawn horizontally into the belly of the cambered masts which, without shrouds or stays, revolved on bearing rings built into the upper and main decks. Like all well-designed ships, she looked smaller than her 52,800 tons and 195 metres overall length suggested; when one became used to the novelty, she *did* look right. She was close-hauled, and, by the two black cones jerking on the bunt of her fore tops'l, she was using her engines. The Spaniard, *Reina de la Mar*, was close astern of her and would be overhauling when clear of the channel. Captain Jones pulled down his cap firmly and walked to the port side.

Less than half a mile on *Windrose's* port bow, Barrett Reef was frothing white: *Windrose* would leave it three cables to port and then could set sail, close-hauled on the starboard tack. He turned aft to check on the ship astern, following at two cables, the pretty three-masted barque, the Polish *Wicher*. She was going well and in a moment of elation, Barnaby raised his cap to her, waving it above his head. It was moments like these which made it all worthwhile and took his mind from the worries of his shipping company. Thank God his partner,

Gavin McBinney, was a hard-headed Scot: back in the Company's Glasgow office, he'd be coping with the disturbing reports in the *Financial Times*, the copy of which Barnaby Jones had given to Jason Mercer.

In turning back to the Pelorus to check the heading, Jones glanced to starboard instinctively, whence danger lurked. He stopped in his tracks, for *Techno Victory* was, unbelievably, swinging to port. Her cones were being rapidly hauled down and her yards were trimming to the wind as she paid off. She would just clear the reef to seaward, but was on collision course with *Windrose*, and *Victory* had right of way, under sail on the starboard tack. For an instant, Barnaby Jones watched through his glasses the figures on the dynaship's bridge. One officer stood on his own, the huge ginger-bearded man who was doffing his cap to *Windrose*. Barnaby recognized plainly the swash-buckling but formidable Randy Buckle, who, from the beginning, had treated all other competitors with contempt.

Windrose could not turn to starboard, for fear of hitting *Reina de la Mar*. Jones dared not alter far to port for fear of menacing *Wicher*, who was overhauling astern. There was only one chance: he would have to risk the reef where the seas threshed two and a half cables off his port bow.

'Full astern together,' he commanded. 'Port fifteen…'

Deck Boy Cyril Plomer was 'two blocks'. He was the weather hand on the main upper topsail yard, and he was numb with cold. The Antarctic wind was penetrating even the double-layered anoraks which McBinney and Jones provided for their crews. Bracing against the footrope and maintaining one hand for himself, 'one hand for the Queen, the other for yourself', they'd always taught him, he stuck the other beneath his armpit. He'd been an idiot in committing the cardinal sin:

showing off by coming aloft without gloves. His mum, cosy in their Birkenhead home, would have berated him for not wearing the mitts she had knitted. Then, mind dulled from the cold and boredom of waiting up here, Cyril Plomer absorbed without interest the other world gyrating wildly beneath him.

The other ships looked like the plastic toys his sister gave her children in the bath. *Windrose* seemed to be surrounded by a flotilla of rivals, each with its creaming wash. From up here, 30 metres above the water, some of those midget ships seemed too close for his liking: that dynaship, *Windrose*'s main rival, was even easing off the wind. Cyril Plomer could see the track of her wake beginning to snake to port. 'She'll be cutting across our bows,' he muttered. 'Silly sod.' What could you expect? Ashore, *Techno Victory*'s crew were a loud-mouthed lot ... just piss and wind.

Then, all of eighteen years, he suddenly felt elated to be here, halfway along a yard and jerking about like a yo-yo: *Windrose* was a taut ship commanded by a disciplinarian and a fine seaman. She was a 'beaut' in a seaway but a cow under power only. The 'outward' race had shaken them down and turned them into seamen: he had quickly mastered his fear of going aloft in the gales. Plomer turned his head to the westward: God, what, for Pete's sake, was *Victory* doing?

He was mesmerized by the sight of the two great sailing ships being sucked together, as if by magnetism. The distance between them was diminishing with each second, and then the yard was suddenly vibrating along its length. He cocked his head sideways to peer downwards, an action he always resisted. As he stared down between his legs, the ship quivered from stem to stern, jolted hard to port. For that one moment, he had failed to concentrate, had loosened his grip...

Mercifully for Cyril Plomer, the next few moments passed swiftly: losing his footing on the footrope, the sudden, unnatural ship's motion jerked him from the yard. Down he plummeted, like a dummy flung from a Hollywood clifftop, towards the threshing sea. The curling waves spiralled towards him, whirling, larger, greener, the confused waters leaping closer … closer.

CHAPTER FOUR: PARTING OF THE WAYS

Jason Mercer found a stool in the port after-corner of *Sherrilee*'s bridge. The aerofoil wind ship was three miles south of Barrett Reef and was on course to leave Cape Palliser two miles to port. The Captain's steward had produced a cup of coffee, and for a few minutes Jason could relax and re-read the city gossip in the *Financial Times* which he had found on board.

The whole of these past fifteen hours seemed unreal. At his age, he was reasonably hardened to violence by his sea-faring life, but what he had experienced during the early hours of this Sunday morning was nightmarish. The wretched James Mirson was a ghastly sight, the fishes having completed the awful mutilation perpetrated by his assassins. After the identification, an immediate preliminary police enquiry was held on board. Afterwards, Jason had been unable to sleep, several unanswered questions turning over and over in his shocked mind. If, as it was suggested, the murder was a case of wrong identification, and mistaken name, why should the opposition go to such lengths to rub out Jason Mercer? If it *was* a 'hit' job by Stok's mafia-like organization, why the need to eliminate or warn off a junior Race Observer? When finally at five thirty he had dropped off, the ensuing nightmares jerked him spasmodically to wakefulness until dawn.

The police had allowed *Sherrilee* to proceed to her start anchorage, but any witnesses might be recalled to Wellington once the race was ended. The authorities were remaining noncommittal, but to Jason (from what Barnaby Jones had told him last night and from the attempted murder of them both) in the clear light of dawn, the assassins' objective was becoming horribly clear: every trick would be used to ensure that a Stok ship won SACOR. The faceless, hired villains would stop at nothing, terrorizing and intimidating all the way to guarantee that Global Sea Transport ships were among the winners. Surely this column, in the City Shipping News of the *Financial Times*, was linked, however remotely? Jason read:

Our city Representative hears from sources which have always proved reliable that it is the Akroyd Stok Consortium which is behind GST's bid for the controlling shares of McBinney and Jones, the small and, because so efficient, valuable shipping firm of Ocean Shipping Company. It is, I regret to report, the old story: the whale swallowing the minnow. I am pleased to announce that Mr Gavin McBinney tells me he is fighting for the company's life.

Jason was refolding the newspaper when the Port Wave began crackling from the loudspeaker on the bulkhead.

'PAN-PAN-PAN... This is *Windrose*, position two cables from Barrett Reefs. Man overboard, *man over...*'

The distress signal cut through the murmur of conversation. The buffeting of the wind against the bridge windows was all that could be heard in the silence. After a pause, Barnaby's slight burr cut in again: 'This is *Windrose*, *Windrose*, *Windrose*: casualty one and a half cables, western edge of Barrett Reef, two-four-o. Request immediate helicopter assistance. I am standing by, clear of reef... OUT.'

The Port Wave operator replied immediately in his Kiwi voice, calm and matter-of-fact: 'Helicopter on its way: Port Signal Station has sight of casualty. Keep clear, please, *Windrose*... OUT.'

Captain Klosson was already outside in the port wing, but *Sherrilee's* bridge team could see little, save *Windrose* bucking in the confused seas off the reef. The whiter-than-white sails of *Techno Victory* were revolving to the wind as the big dynaship went about to the port tack. She looked close to *Windrose* but was taking no part in the emergency. She was heading for Sinclair Head, presumably to make to windward before tacking again for the open ocean. *Sherrilee's* officer of the watch was poking his head through the port doorway: 'Pencarrow Head abeam to port, Cap'n.'

'Bring her round,' Klosson bawled above the wind. 'Set course for Chatham Island and tell the navigator.'

'Aye, aye, sir.'

'And trim the sails...'

'This is Port Nicholson calling *Windrose*,' the loudspeaker announced from the bulkhead. 'Helicopter has sighted casualty. Stay clear... OUT.'

Jason spotted the tiny dot scraping the scudding clouds. It was hovering close to *Windrose*, who was half-obliterated by the spume from the angry seas off the reef. He saw the wire going down with a brave man on the end of it ... then the dangling rescuer disappearing into the swirling waters.

The silence on *Sherrilee's* bridge was broken only by the officer of the watch's orders to the helmsman and the crackling from the loudspeaker. Then up through the boiling seas the casualty and his rescuer appeared. Even from here, four miles away, everyone on *Sherrilee's* bridge was holding his breath until the two dangling shapes were swallowed into the chopper's belly. Lurching sideways, tail up, the machine spiralled off towards Strathmore Park.

'This is Port Nicholson radio calling *Windrose*. Casualty is suffering from severe exposure and is being taken to

Wellington General Hospital. His self-inflating jacket saved him, but he's in a critical condition, Captain… OVER.'

In came Barnaby again, his voice as steady as ever: 'This is *Windrose, Windrose, Windrose*. Thank you, Port Nicholson radio. Please thank chopper pilot and crew. I'd like an early report on casualty's condition, please… OVER.'

'Okay, Captain. What are your intentions?'

'Proceeding for Horn passage. Will maintain radio watch on 2182 for arrangements regarding Ordinary Seaman Plomer… OUT.'

While *Sherrilee*'s bridge team returned to the shelter of the wheelhouse, Jason watched the great barque setting sail. First the fore upper topsail, followed by the main's and the mizzen's; then out broke two foresails. She bent to the wind and, even under reduced canvas, seemed to be revelling in her longed-for element; she was breath-takingly beautiful. So Captain Jones was not wasting time over an incident he could not affect. He was allowing the port authorities no latitude to hold him; and Jason could picture the craggy-faced old man, as stubborn as ever, never deviating from his objective whatever the calamities around him. Presumably they'd fly Plomer to Montevideo. Jason turned back to the warmth of the wheelhouse. Once *Sherrilee* was clear of Turakirae Head, Palliser Bay and the distant Cape Palliser, he would go below to have a look round this fine ship.

Sherrilee was making fourteen knots from her aerofoils and with her engines idling at their most economical speed, but she was on her best point of sailing, with the wind broad on the bow. Perhaps by the time he had finished his tour (the Exec. Franklin Dicker had volunteered to take him round), Captain Klosson might declare which passage the ship was making. Chatham Island would be coming up tomorrow during the afternoon watch, and by then everyone would know whom they were up against. He unzipped his anorak as he stepped over the door's coaming and shivered, feeling the Antarctic wind. He tried to shake off the sense of foreboding which was eating into him. The race had begun ominously for, according to the RO's report, *Techno Victory* had made a deliberately aggressive move in crossing *Windrose*'s bow like that. If Jason knew anything about Barnaby Jones, far from being intimidated by these monstrous assaults on him, the old seadog would himself declare war against his giant adversary.

ACHTUNG!

Alles Touristen Und Non-technischen Looken Peepers! Das Machine control is Nicht Fur Gurfingerpoken Und Miteen-grabben. Oder-wise is Easy Schnappen Der Springeniverk, Blowenfuse, Und Poppencorken Mit Spitzen-sparken. Der Machine is Diggen by Experten Only. Is Nicht Fur Gerverken by Das Dumm-kopfen. Das Rubbernecken Sightseenen Keepen Das Kottonpicken Hands in Das Pokets, Zo Relaxen Und Watchen Das Blinkenlights

'That's the only way,' Franklin Dicker drawled. 'When our Electrical Engineer first joined, we were plagued by compulsive knob-pushers.' Then, chuckling to himself, he walked out of the Refrigeration Control Computer Room and began his conducted tour of *Sherrilee*.

Having seen the amazing complexity of controlling different temperatures in each of the 1,600 container boxes, two hours later Dicker and Jason emerged on to the upper deck. The red sun hung above the western horizon, which was lit by a brassy glow; gold, shot by streaks of leaden crimson, like congealing blood. Jason shivered as they stared at the ships silhouetted against that mysterious orb which was drawing down the curtain on this unforgettable day. Above their heads the after 'sail' was creaking, the wind sighing eerily through the slots in the fibre-glass vanes. It was difficult to credit that the contraptions rearing thirty-two metres above the deck were adding such a contribution to the big ship's progress. With the wind forty degrees on *Sherrilee*'s starboard bow, the aerofoils were being automatically held there in Mode Two by their own computer which was a box of less than a cubic foot. At the same time the revs on the main engines, again through the computer, were being reduced automatically as the 'sails' provided the extra forward thrust. There was a lumpy sea from the south: the sails were damping down the ship's motion to a remarkable extent and she was listing to only four degrees.

'Just like a sailboat,' Dicker said. 'We've been able to economize in the building: no stabilizers needed in a Wind Ship.'

They moved up to the bridge through the accommodation island. From up here they could pick out the ships spread across the horizon.

'Last time we'll see 'em all together,' murmured Dicker. 'Perhaps the Old Man'll tell us soon which way we're going.'

'Due east and slap down the middle still,' the Navigating Officer murmured. 'We'll sink Chatham Island if we carry on like this until tomorrow night.'

Franklin Dicker picked up his binoculars while Jason checked off the ships against his list of entrants. 'Jeez, the French Cat's a beaut...!'

'*Rêve de l'Avenir*,' Jason checked. 'Who's that this side of the Frenchman?'

'The Italian. Can't you see her kites? *Stella Venus*.'

The ducted fan-ship was an amazing sight: a massive bow wave was splashing at her bulbous bow as her kites scraped the clouds and tugged at her erratically.

'I'll take the northern lot first,' Dicker called. 'The fleshpot-squaddies for Panama.'

First came the Flettner rotor ships, interspersed with the windmills who in this beam wind were slowly giving place to the grotesque rotor ships: the third in line, *Californian Rose*, the big American, gave an impression of power with her two huge, vertical turbines. She was followed by the French *eólienne Jacques-Yves Cousteau*; *Techno Phanta*, Stok's third candidate, brought up the rear in this gaggle. The big boys, *Niger*, *Ocean Kite* and *Hijaz*, in that order, were the last and strung distantly along the horizon.

The majority of the Horn contingent were already diverging southwards and merging into the darkness of the higher latitudes, as if announcing that they preferred their own company, whatever the dangers. *Techno Victory*'s sails were prominent against the gloom and, even at this distance, Jason could see her listing to the wind and scything through the seas. He turned aft, towards the sunset, to search for Barnaby Jones. Dicker shouted, binoculars pressed into his eye sockets: 'There she is, there's *Windrose*...'

He handed the glasses to Jason. 'Limeys always lose the first battles, don't they, Mercer?' He paused to allow Jason to pick up the barque. A smudge on the horizon: even in the fading twilight, he could see that she had set all sail, except for her royals.

'Guess the dynaship's got it tucked away now,' Dicker said. 'She's going well.'

'*Techno Victory*'s untried,' Jason said quietly. '*Windrose* is a proven ship; she'll stand anything.'

'Anything? Don't taunt The Horn, Mercer. *Victory* looks good to me.'

'Maybe, just now,' Jason replied. 'The leaches of her sails are still unstretched. They completely resuited her in Wellington.'

'How come, Mercer?'

'Her performance depends upon the aerofoil shape of her sails,' Jason said, sensitive to the sceptics on the bridge. 'No one has yet made an unstretchable soft sail. If you get a slack leach on the sail, you lose your aerofoil effect. There's no way you can take up the slack on the leach. Unless *Victory* springs a surprise,' Jason added, 'once her leaches have stretched and she comes on the wind, she'll have a lot of dirty linen hanging up there... We'll see.' The navigation lights were gleaming and frost was already forming on the upperworks when Dicker led the way back into the wheelhouse. Captain Klosson was standing in the centre of his control complex.

'Well, gentlemen,' he said. 'I guess no one can see us now,' and he glanced sardonically at them all. 'Starboard ten, bring her round to 1450.'

The compass strip clicked rhythmically to the new course. *Sherrilee* steadied and the first genuine Pacific roller smothered the fo'c'sle.

Franklin Dicker was grinning. 'I've always had a yen for becoming a "Horner", Cap'n. I guess *Siddartho Maru* will be feeling lonely tomorrow.' The radio room phone bleeped and the officer of the watch answered it. He turned to the master.

'That British seaman has died, sir. Exposure.'

Klosson stared at Jason, pursed his lips and nodded his head. '*Windrose* seems to be unlucky, Mr Mercer,' he said in his mid-Westerner's drawl. 'A killer: yes, sir, a killer ship...' Turning on his heel, he pushed through the after door which led to his cabin.

Dicker was the first to reach the chart table, where the navigator was spreading out the chart. The Great Circle course traced south-east to The Horn.

'The Screaming Fifties, Exec.,' he said, looking up at them all. 'It'll be interesting to see how our sails stand up to wind, snow and ice.'

CHAPTER FIVE: THE SCREAMING FIFTIES

First light was breaking to the eastward when, at 0705 on the next morning, Monday, 24 June, Jason Mercer looked out from the port wing of *Sherrilee*'s bridge. Slamming the sliding door behind him, he crouched double to avoid the spume flying up from the port quarter as the ship corkscrewed before the running sea. And as the new day gradually took over from the fading twilight, he searched the vastness of that huge ocean through his binoculars. Abeam, where the radar blip had showed to the north, were two white blotches, separated one from the other by less than a knuckle's width: the topsails of two square-riggers. They were hull-down and the leading ship, her sails whiter than the other, was probably the dynaship, *Techno Victory*: her masts were the tallest of all the dynaships, even higher than the Costa Rican, *Red Star*, that giant with her Russian officers and mixed crew. Ten minutes later, the mastheads were invisible and Jason was left alone while dawn crept in from the east.

Right ahead, the bands of sweeping cloud were slashed crimson by the sun which was already spreading its frigid light upon the leaden wastes. From horizon to horizon, the endless 'greybeards', as the seamen of the Windjammers used to call these cohorts of huge waves, surged onwards. Down on the latitude of Sixty South there was no land mass to hinder this gigantic swell from revolving eternally around the Southern Pole. These waves, this swell, Jason mused, contained specks of cosmic energy originating from the beginnings of the world when the seas had covered the planet.

The vastness of this ocean humbled a man: it was over 5,000 nautical miles to The Horn and the Drake Passage; 6,000 to Vancouver, 7,000 to Panama ... but, relatively, this mysterious continent of Antarctica was very close. Cape Adare and *Discovery*'s original base (Captain Scott was one of Jason's greatest heroes) lay only 1,300 miles to the south, and in a little over a week's time *Sherrilee* would be due north of the bases and territories which Chile, Argentine and the Soviets now claimed for themselves.

Only too swiftly had the international idealism of scientists been submerged by politics. The politicians were now prostituting the Antarctic: Chileans and Argentinians glared at each other from their military bases; the Russians had built massive fuel storage facilities for their submarines in their deep-water bases at Bellinghausen. There was not much doubt why Port Stanley was so vital to the British and the free world. The cat-and-mouse game continued remorselessly as man lusted after the untapped mineral and vegetable wealth of Antarctica. Jason moved into the wind to read the ship's heading from the gyro-repeater: the course was still 145 degrees. Surprisingly, *Sherrilee* was heading well south of The Horn.

'Morning, Jason: first time on this little pond?'

Franklin Dicker was standing shivering behind him, his head protruding through the door. 'Hey, come inside. Are all you Limeys masochists?' He was shaved and was wearing a cap and the company uniform. Captain Klosson did not take a watch, and there were four Mates. Dicker, the jovial Mate, had taken over from the Second and was sweeping the horizon with his binoculars.

'Reckon that leading ship was *Techno Victory*,' he murmured, while he checked aloud the names of the ships who had been sighted yesterday steering The Horn route. The names were inscribed on a chinagraph board below the wind shield of each bridge wing:

Windrose
Techno Victory
Sao Isabel
Sea Falcon
Yankee Flyer
Stella Venus
Pollux
Amazone
Wicher
Rêve de l'Avenir
Ocean Kite
Dynasaur
Siddartho Maru and the Spanish Cruise Clipper, *Reina de la Mar.*

'It'll be interesting to see who comes off best between that Stok dynaship and the five-masted barque,' Franklin Dicker said. 'Anybody's guess, I reckon.' He glanced ahead through the windows at *Sherrilee*'s aerofoil sails. 'I've got used to 'em. Don't notice the noise now,' he commented.

The two five-vaned aerofoils, each on its mast for'd and aft, were jerking in half-degree steps as they maintained their optimum angle to the apparent wind. Their buff, glass fibre sails were glistening from the spindrift which was reaching even to the heads of the sails. Because the wind was dead astern and edging up to Force 8, the aerofoil sails remained within the normal operating range: to produce the maximum forward thrust the computer was controlling in 30-second 'steps', the angle of the vanes to the apparent wind. She was steering so well that the Captain had shut down the engines and she was running solely under windpower. It was also comforting to see, between the fore aerofoil and the stump foremast on the fo'c'sle-head, the small mast carrying the vertical-axis turbine generator: if the ship ever lost all power, this wind turbine could provide enough electricity to run the wind sails, and to sail the ship out of danger.

Sherrilee was now entirely under sail, a unique experience for Jason. 25,300 tons and barely yawing, this wind sail ship was completely under control as she surged up the slopes of the Antarctic swell. She carried two smaller diesels rather than one large unit, an economy which was made possible by the wind sails; and with her propeller now fully feathered, she was bowling along at eleven knots before the wind.

From the bridge Jason's vision was unimpaired by the sails, for the foremast aerofoil was set twenty feet higher to prevent the bridge being 'wooded' when she was pitching. The problem of masking the radar by the aerofoil had been solved by fixing the main set high up on the foremast. Without the engines, the ship was strangely silent; there was no vibration and only the pounding of the seas shook the hull. This was a unique ship with an amazingly economical system. She came from an American stable, but the British were in the game too: the Walker Wingsail was fitted in *Niger*, who was Panama-bound.

Jason preferred *Sherrilee* in this Mode 4, with her sails stalled to give as much drag as possible. Klosson was 'goose-winging' her to see if this would reduce her sheer up to windward. Not only had he succeeded, but this posture also reduced her yawing. The sails made a great difference when the wind was abeam and, though carrying a four-degree list, her rolling was dramatically reduced. *Sherrilee* was more sea-kindly, thanks to her wind sails, than any ship of a comparable size in which Jason had sailed, but he wondered what effect those towering sails would have on her stability when, soon now, she must do battle with the dreaded weather of The Horn. He turned to Franklin Dicker, who must have been reading his mind.

'We should start to run down our Easting in three days' time,' said the Exec. 'Next Thursday night ... the twenty-seventh of June. The Captain's keen to stay clear of the others by keeping well south. Our old *Sherrilee*'s already proved herself in a seaway.'

'Captain Klosson judges the ice hazard as less of a risk than collision with the other ships?' Jason ventured. 'How far south is he taking her?'

'The fifty-eighth parallel. Our main radar should pick up the growlers okay, though the ice is reported higher north this year.'

Jason kept his thoughts to himself. When he had once been round The Horn in the old *Port Pirie*, her Captain had been more wary of the ice than the appalling weather. A growler, though only a broken-off lump from an iceberg, could slice a lethal hole in a ship's side.

'The Old Man likes to play safe, Jason. Even with Satnav and radio time signals, longitude can still be unreliable. He'll round up for Montevideo when Staten Island is due north of us. We'll cross the Drake Passage and the West Wind Drift will take us clear of Staten until the Falkland Current takes us on northwards.'

A comforting thought, mused Jason. During the Windjammer era, ships had piled up on the Auckland and Campbell Islands, south of New Zealand, when wrong with their longitude. Masters preferred to sail along safe latitudes: an occasional noon meridian altitude sight which gave a latitude was a simpler job than a longitude position based on a single unreliable chronometer. Sailormen still yarned of the *General Grant* who sailed from Melbourne in 1866; carrying gold dust and forty-five passengers, she drifted against the sheer cliffs of Auckland Island and was wrecked. She was sucked into a cave, the swell causing her mastheads to strike against the roof of the dark cavern until the mast steps were hammered through the keelson. Crashing rocks from the roof of the cave plummeted upon the decks; not one lifeboat got away without capsizing as they tried to clear the surf swirling past the entrance to the cave. The stewardess was among the ten survivors who scrambled up the cliffs to live on seal meat, birds and goats until, after many ordeals, they were rescued by chance a year and a half later.

Eighty years earlier, when the first steam-driven vessel in Britain made her maiden voyage on a Scottish loch, another brave ship, commanded by another Scot, Captain John Hunter, made an historic voyage in an effort to save the starving colony of New South Wales. Being given by the Governor the leaking five-hundred-ton *Sirius*, Hunter was told to sail west across the southern Indian ocean to acquire provisions from Cape Town. But the Scottish Captain, having already experienced the continuous westerlies across the Indian ocean, decided to chance his arm and instead of battling against headwinds, he sailed his rotten ship eastabout, two-thirds round the world and past Cape Horn. The 'brave west winds' (the Roaring Forties) drove him on his epic voyage and he saved the colony; years later, he himself became Governor of New South Wales.

What men those seamen were, surpassing even the Windjammer crews in courage and endurance! And Jason, having completed the details of the ship's position and engine hours for his Race Observer's log, left the bridge. At midday *Sherrilee* had crossed the International Date Line. She picked up Bounty Island on radar, but failed to sight either it or the Antipodes Islands. Jason could sense a feeling of excitement in the ship: at last she was really on her way.

Thirteen days later, it was the difference in *Sherrilee*'s motion which woke Jason Mercer. She was yawing so violently that he could no longer sleep and, taking advantage of the early watchkeeper's breakfast, he clambered to the bridge. His liking of Franklin Dicker seemed to be mutual, but the Exec. was not yet on the bridge, so Jason had time to study the chart at the after end of the wheelhouse:

Monday, 8 July: ship's Dead Reckoning for her noon position 58° South 62° 58' West; fifteen days out from Wellington and making good twelve knots under her aerofoil 'sails'.

At noon, the Navigator laid off the new course, north to the eastern tip of Staten Island which would take the ship across the swell; and presumably the West Wind Drift would take her well clear of land during her northing across the notorious Drake Passage. Jason was surprised that Klosson had not already tried to ease *Sherrilee* across these huge, following seas, but at that moment the officer of the watch, the Second Mate, picked up the engine room telephone.

'Thanks, Chief. I'll ask the Captain.'

When the Second returned from the Old Man's cabin, he carried out the steering breakdown drill with the Bo'sun's Mate, by changing over to 'hand' for a moment; he then handed over the watch to the Exec. Once the watch had settled down and during that quarter of an hour before the Captain was expected to appear on the bridge, Franklin Dicker primed his friend on the day's routine.

'I want to get the crew on deck,' he confided to Jason. 'But the Old Man won't hear of it in this…' He jerked his head towards the seas surging past the port wing outside. 'I should have thought of it earlier,' Dicker said. 'S'pose the Old Man's right.'

'Skippers always are,' Jason said, and a sardonic smile creased Franklin Dicker's open face.

'Have you seen the Weatherfax, Jason? The barometer's dropping already and I wanted to double-up on the lashings and securing chains.' Together they stared at the container boxes, stacked almost to bridge level and stretching forward between the aerofoil masts. The ship was lunging down the troughs, her stern cocked up like a toy boat's, as she careered down the mountain side … down, down … then the corkscrew yawing, the spray flying high and enveloping the for'd sails.

'It's gonna blow,' Franklin said. 'Blow like hell. Force twelve plus; the weathermen aren't often wrong.'

Jason whistled softly. 'It's been Force eight and nine for the last fortnight: I've almost got used to it.' They remained silent, each with his thoughts. Even a ship of this size could be tossed about on this ocean like a speck of seaweed. Jason remained on the bridge until the daily Race Positions were sent up by the radio office. All the ships on The Horn passage were giving only an 'estimated position': the Navigator had not been able to take a noon sunsight since Chatham Island because of cloud and low visibility.

Having decided not to risk The Horn after trouble with the main deck bearings of her ducted fan, *Stella Venus* was making for the Strait of Magellan; the German, *Amazone*, was the only windmill braving The Horn, *Yankee Flyer* and *Ocean Kite* being the only kite ships. The RFA dynaship, *Pollux*, was taking the Magellan Strait after broaching-to, following rudder failure. *Siddartho Maru*, *Sherrilee*'s rival, had radioed whether the shipyard in Punta Arena could undertake upper deck repairs, but there was no hint yet which route she was taking. The remainder, including all the square riggers and the big American schooner, *Sea Falcon*, were forcing on towards The Horn. Little *Wicher*, the Pole, had already rounded up and was making for Staten Island. Jason could imagine the tension in her as she ran for the lee of Tierra del Fuego before the storm hit her.

Windrose seemed to be six hours astern of *Techno Victory*, whose position was reported as thirty-seven miles north of *Sherrilee*'s. The Navigator had been down to the radio office and succeeded in obtaining a second class DF bearing on the great dynaship. For her position at 0800, she reported typically that she was doing twenty-one knots and hoping for more. Jason glanced at the greybeards sliding past the port windows, took a quick look at the barometer, then went below. He'd catch up on his work before the motion became worse: he still had not taken the forenoon readings to enter in his log.

CHAPTER SIX: THE HORN

Jason Mercer returned to the bridge just after nine: the barometer had fallen an inch during that past hour. Captain Klosson was huddled morosely in his chair, shoulders hunched and watching his ship. As soon as the Weatherfax came in, he decided to try and make for the lee of Staten Island, but there were 240 miles to cover before the storm struck. He had set the fore 'sail' for a broad reach on the port track, the after sail in Mode One, the quiescent position. He had set half ahead on his engines, but the steering was barely holding her from broaching-to. Klosson had stronger nerves than his officers: there were moments which caused Jason to hold his breath, when she rolled on to her huge slab side as the great swells lifted her bodily. Then the ocean seemed to slide away beneath her and, as she rolled, she would sheer viciously to windward, into those foaming torrents of dark breakers somersaulting over themselves, where they burst down from the mountainous heights astern of *Sherrilee*'s poop.

The helm had long been changed over to 'hand' and the best Quartermaster was now on the steering, the control lever in his hand. For long seconds he was standing there, legs astride, a dour, balding, gum-chewing mid-Westerner, his eyes fixed on the compass tape as it ticked remorselessly up to windward, while his control button remained over at hard-a-starboard. As the Captain watched the rudders and their indicators, the silence as the controls remained 'hard over' was punctuated only by the crashing of the seas pounding outside.

This is a strange world, mused Jason. Inside, all the comfort of a modern bridge. Warm, heated by electricity from the diesel generators; dry, with anti-misting devices to prevent the steaming-up of the reinforced windows; clear-view circles of glass whirling steadily ahead of the officer of the watch; and the Old Man glaring at the spume spouting upwards and drifting in clouds four hundred feet from her plunging bows. Klosson, sucking his peppermints and smacking his lips in that mannerism of his (like a whale blowing, thought Jason), would climb from his chair every half hour and, grabbing the handholds, lurch to the thin barometer tube swinging vertically on its gimbles in the port after-corner of the wheelhouse. Then, shaking his head, he would slide across to the radar where, ostrich-like, he would submerge into the visor: rather pointless in this appalling weather, it seemed to Jason Mercer.

At 0945, the radar red lamp flickered briefly and the alert buzzer sounded. A blip glowed intermittently on the north-easterly bearing; the echo was faint, impossible to range: the set was on long scale, for Staten was another world away and the nearest ship, *Techno Victory*, estimated seventy miles to the northward … but how others were faring now, no one cared. Each ship was fighting for herself, survival paramount.

Windrose was heard briefly on the air at 1010, her distorted sentences impossible to understand. The voice bore the steady tones of Captain Jones: up here among men who were not his own countrymen, Jason felt a close kinship flowing out to that sturdy man now fighting for his ship's survival to the northward — how many miles off, no one knew, for Barnaby had been keeping things close to his chest.

There was nothing else to think about now, nothing save the pandemonium of the storm, which was mounting hourly in ferocity. By 1030 the glass had fallen to 27.70 and by noon, when the Navigator made a facetious remark about his Mer. Alt., the reading was 27.40. Never had Jason experienced such a depression and, judging by the strained look on everyone's faces, nor had anyone else. The steward managed to produce hot soup, and then Jason slipped out of the starboard doorway to see for himself whether there was worse to come.

The wind was now screaming through the upperworks, the anemometer fluttering between 80 and 90 knots. Waves the size of three-storey houses were bounding astern, climbing, building higher and higher, with streamers of overhanging crests snarling above *Sherrilee*'s mainmast. There they would hang for an instant, poised to smother the puny, man-made ship; then, down the combers foamed in an area the size of a tennis court as they curled towards the ship. The birds had disappeared long ago, to shelter in the troughs until the storm was over.

The sky was a swirling, indigo fury, the base of the streaming clouds lunging to embrace the leaping seas. But it was the noise, the overwhelming, thunderous roar of those towering seas which struck terror into men's hearts. No one among even these tough, modern, seafaring men had sailed through anything like this before. Jason watched as a mountainous wall of water, dark against the leaping western horizon, began building higher and higher astern of *Sherrilee*'s transom.

Her stern lifted. Down went her forefoot, then the whole ship, 25,000 tons of her, skidding down the steep slopes and into the foam-streaked trough of the valley … down, down like a tiny toy boat, into the boiling maelstrom. Jason held on to the protection rail, unable to tear his eyes away from this monstrous wall of water about to engulf the vessel. Then, as *Sherrilee* dipped her stern to start the uphill swoop, the crest broke, smothering the poop deck. The seas flung inboard, and there was a cascade of foaming, roaring waters; the *crack!* of timber; the shock of shattering fibre-glass. And as the mountain of green water swept onwards and forwards into the container deck, all that Jason could see of the starboard lifeboat was an orange, twisted hull, crushed like a broken egg, hanging from the after davit. The rest of the boat was in pieces, the for'd falls stranded and parted, the blocks torn from the hog. Slamming the door behind him, he glimpsed the ferocious sea smashing onwards, foaming and leaping across the tops of the deck containers.

'Don't want too many of those, Exec.!' the Captain yelled above the roaring confusion. 'She's a sturdy ol' girl, ain't she?'

Jason could not catch Franklin's reply because the 'alert' buzzer was hooting from the main radar. The red light glowed from the set, flickered, faded... The ship was poised on the summit of a colossal wave but then began once more her crazy slide downwards into the valley. Wallowing at the bottom, then out to the next ascent again, to the crest and its precipice. No radar blip, nothing on the screen... The traces were revolving normally, their slim fingers probing the fluorescent screen which showed only clutter from the raging storm.

'Must have been *Techno Victory*'s echo,' Klosson yelled. 'Keep an eye open for her, Officer of the Watch.'

And as the forenoon merged into afternoon, the air around the ship grew warmer. Condensation was beginning to smear the windows, so they pushed up the heating to clear the glass. The Bo'sun's Mate was wiping the midship window, when he dropped his bucket. Stabbing at the thick pane, he yelled: 'Cap'n... RIGHT AHEAD!'

Heads jerked upwards; faces pressed against the windows. Jason could see only long lines of glistening container tops as *Sherrilee* pitched down the long, watery slope.

'Hard a-port! Stop port engine...!'

Jason's breath was fogging the dense plate in front of him as his eyes strained to sight the orange hull and its violet upperworks bucking in the confused seas. He was searching for her spade-like masts...

There must have been at least a quarter of a mile between the peaks of these huge swells lunging around the South Pole. The puny *Sherrilee* was crawling from the pit of one of these troughs, and as she began to lift before the mountains of water tumbling down upon her from astern, her bows scything the black waters beneath her forefoot, Jason saw it. He blinked; his eyes were tired. He was seeing things...

There, on the next summit, was a vague shadow, impossible to identify in the spume of the leaping horizon. It hung there, ethereal at the peak of the swell, glistening grey-green until, where it had fused with the water, its sinister underwater mass disappeared beneath the sea. As the spectre began sliding down upon *Sherrilee*, it yawed towards her, plunging with awful, regular rhythm into the seas. With each second that passed, the ghost materialized more definitely into the murderous danger it was. And as the ship began to swing to port across the swell swooping upon her from astern, the bearing of the sixty-feet-high chunk of iceberg began slowly to draw aft.

Franklin Dicker was flinging himself at the 'collision' alarm button. And as the iceberg, so close that Jason could almost lean out and touch it, slid abeam and began to draw aft towards the starboard quarter, Klosson snatched the steering control himself and shoved it hard over to starboard.

'Stop starboard. Full ahead port.'

It must have been too late. The peak of the iceberg was on a level with *Sherrilee*'s bridge; then, riding beneath the wing, it listed slowly away from *Sherrilee*'s side. And as the mortal menace rolled away, the underside swung upwards, its knifelike fangs stabbing upwards at the ship's hull to slice her open like a sardine tin.

'Hold on, for God's sake! Brace yourselves…'

It was Franklin who shouted the warning. And as they stood squarely against the ship's lurch to starboard, she rolled her bottom away, away from those stiletto needles. Then, as the ship veered to port across the swell again, the transparent green monster ducked steadily aft, off the starboard quarter. Up and up it reared, dithered an instant at the top of the next swell … then disappeared for ever.

The ship was now reaching the top of the mountain and, as she clung to the summit with her rudders still hard a-starboard, the breaking crest struck her starboard quarter. *Sherrilee* was no longer a ship, but a bauble tossed by giant hands on to her beam ends. She lay over, her port gunwales underwater while millions of tons of sea smothered her.

The lights dimmed. Bells started ringing. A roaring was all about them as Jason clung to the lip of an open drawer to avoid being smashed into the melee on the other side. She hung there, this great ship, poised between life and death. She was shuddering the length of her, the deck vibrating like a banjo string.

'*God save us*!' The words sprang from Jason's lips.

Then, slowly he found himself sitting upright, as she began to right herself. She crossed the vertical, rolled to starboard, then catapulted back to port. She was floating still, her bows paying off to port from the blow of the rogue sea. This was the stroke of fortune which saved her.

As she was sliding down out of control into the trough again, the port engine coughed back to life. Klosson reversed the helm, and slowly regained control. But the devastation for'd was beyond belief.

The securing chains of the for'd port container must have parted. A bright red 'box' was half up-ended and wedged across the for'd aerofoil mast. The other boxes around the displaced container were jumbled in a heap, like a pack of cards. *Sherrilee*'s bows were being borne down by the force of the for'd sail which, instead of being trimmed in the quiescent mode and idling, was jammed and presenting the greatest sail area possible.

Klosson snatched at the strident telephone. 'Bridge — computer room? Yes, Captain… *What…?* Jammed on Green one-one-eight? Well, you fool, un-jam it!' Klosson was flushed with fury as he slammed the instrument back into its holder. He rounded on his Exec. 'Muster all hands in survival suits up here, Mr Dicker. With that fool sail drawing all it can, I can't turn across the swell, even if I want to. I'll have to try, so stand by the boats.' He snorted, one eye on the crushed remains of the davit.

No boat, thought Jason, *could ever get away in this, let alone survive an instant.*

The Captain was yelling at Jeff Hines, his Second, the dour New Jerseyman. 'Pass our position to the Radio Officer. Tell Sparks to make out a preparatory PAN-PAN-PAN for Radio Falkland … just in case, Mr Hines.'

Neither Hines nor Jason could clearly hear the Captain's words. He was fighting for his wildly yawing ship, as she slithered down the long slope of the swell. He was increasing the revolutions on the starboard engine to half-ahead to prevent her from broaching-to across the mountainous swell.

Then Jason heard a mounting, roaring sound from astern, like a Jumbo on take-off. With the others, he was watching through the after windows a monstrous phalanx of advancing ocean, dark and towering like a block of flats above *Sherrilee*'s poop deck. The whole of this western horizon seemed to be looming above the ship, a silver strip gleaming on the gigantic swell. Then this endless crest began to unravel and gather speed, spurting and hurtling onwards, leap-frogging and spouting in great jets of foam. And as the fury thundered upon them, the engine-room alarm hooter blared from the pelorus console. At the same instant, the bridge team was galvanized by the impending disaster.

The red glow of a warning lamp was flickering from the control console. The starboard engine had stopped. Now nothing could stop *Sherrilee* from broaching to starboard, across the face of this raging fury. Flattened on her beam-ends, she would be rolled over, now that the boxes had broken loose...

'Tell Sparks to clear the PAN-PAN-PAN,' Klosson bellowed above the bedlam.

CHAPTER SEVEN: VORTEX

When Captain Barnaby Jones noted his officer of the watch's barometer reading for 0800 on Monday, 8 July, he reacted instinctively to the alarm bells ringing inside his brain. The lowering clouds, the rising wind and the Weatherfax bade him order all hands and to shorten sail. While they were reducing to only fore and main topsails, Jones pushed out *Windrose*'s position, then listened to the other ships transmitting theirs. *Techno Victory* came in loud and clear, followed by the aerofoil ship, *Sherrilee*, well to the southward.

Jones had kept his barque further north, preferring to trust to his accurate navigation in avoiding The Horn rather than risk the hazard of ice. He loathed the strain and vigilance required when growlers were loose: a square-rigged ship could not manoeuvre like the motor vessels.

This radio signalling lent a cosiness to the whole scene, however bad the quality of reception. It was good to know that Jason Mercer was off to the southward. There was something homely about having him there, for Barnaby's own daughter seemed to like the young seafarer. The Captain wondered, as he watched his men going aloft, how Hannah was faring near the Equator. *Wandering Star* must be nearing the Galapagos by now, for this was the fifteenth day since the start of the race. A schooner like *Wandering Star* would be at a standstill in light airs, but when she picked up the south-east trade winds broad on her bow, she would swiftly regain much of the distance she had lost.

This other Akroyd Stok ship, *Techno Victory*, was certainly making the most of the media. During the 0800 position report this morning, Buckle's voice had come on the air: twenty-one knots, he claimed, and why should he worry about the ominous forecast? His dynaship was technically unbeatable, with every modern device the marine industry could produce. Not only did he have the usual Satnav and Weatherfax, but also the coded weather-routing direct from Global Sea Transport's Head Office in the Barbican. Obeying computer orders, he was confidently bashing on before the gales. *Victory* was only thirty-five miles to the north and twelve miles ahead.

Barnaby Jones glanced at the gimballed chronometer in *Windrose*'s fibre-glass wheelhouse, a reinforced bridge which he had helped to design himself. Being a belt-and-braces man, he had insisted on this time-keeping instrument, despite Gavin McBinney's indulgent smile. Surely, Gavin had asked, in these days of radio time signals and Satnav satellites, the old-fashioned method of position-finding could be dispensed with for economy's sake? Thank God for Gavin in his unpretentious Glasgow office now, a dependable, loyal partner when Akroyd Stok was baring his teeth...

It was 1030, two hours after the barometer had plummeted, when Barnaby moved back to the instrument for another reading. He whistled softly: 27.70. This depression was developing into a storm of cyclone force. He forced his way through the starboard door and was nearly knocked over by the wind gusting from the starboard quarter.

To the west the sky was leaden, with black clouds scudding the horizon which was barely separated from the leaping seas following astern in endless succession. *Windrose* was flying before the wind and skidding down the ocean's mountain sides. The helmsman was having to use maximum wheel when the sheers came ... and this was the moment when Barnaby

Jones felt the warning touch which all seamen feel at some time in their lives.

He watched his men rolling forward, slithering across the heaving deck. As she humped over the next summit, a breaking crest crashed on board across the starboard quarter. Smashing everything movable, hungry for any man too slow to jump for the lifelines, the foaming sea charged along the deck. And when the cauldron had dispersed itself against the fo'c'sle head, the hands manned the halliards, clewlines and buntlines. Then, a squall thundered down from the west and, with a crack like a gun, the fore upper topsail burst from its boltrope and vanished to leeward. And while the Captain anxiously watched his hands furling the fore lower topsail, he was dimly aware of the radio office loudspeaker gabbling a distorted voice message. The hands were coming down from aloft and Barnaby sighed with relief as he stood over the helmsman to watch how he was coping with the steering. The door at the back of the wheelhouse burst open on the roll to propel Sparks through it. Pale-faced and sleep-hungry, the Radio Officer handed the message to his Captain without comment: 'PAN-PAN-PAN… This is *Techno Victory…*'

Randy Buckle's ship was in trouble. Her diesel alternators were inoperative due to a sea flooding the auxiliary engine room. She was without electrical power until she could get the emergency generator going. The flying spume was freezing on her Teflon-coated glass sails. She was reefing mechanically as fast as she could, but was forced to use hand-power now that her hydraulics were 'off the board'. She gave her estimated position as 88 miles, 065° from Staten Island, which put her twelve miles due north of *Windrose*. Her distress call was timed 1040, but the strength of signal was weak and barely decipherable. Less than a minute later, Barnaby heard through his bridge loudspeaker, Radio Ushuaia coming in, strength 7: help would be on its way as soon as the wind moderated and helicopters could become airborne.

Captain Jones could picture the predicament in which Buckle found himself. *Victory* must be in a bad way and, when things went wrong under these conditions, difficulties compounded with terrifying speed. Barnaby made up his mind: crossing to the chart table, he laid off an interception course towards the dynaship. Without looking up from the chart, he shouted above the wind to the officer of the watch: 'Sweep on radar between 020° and 060°,' he commanded. '*Victory* ought to come up soon.' He turned to Bellew. 'Tell the engine room I'll be needing both engines.'

He staggered across to the controls and pressed both pushes. He felt the vibration beneath his feet, even above the sea's pounding, then eased forward the port throttle. When *Windrose* was running on 'slow port' and ticking over on starboard, he turned to his second-in-command. 'Take over the wheel, Mr Mate. Steer as you've never steered before. Port ten and steady her on 040°. I'll take it in steps.'

Outside there was only the roaring of the wind. If *Windrose* broached now, if the staysail failed to hold her and the engine torque was not enough, she'd be overwhelmed.

It was certainly a job to get your soup during those next few hours in *Windrose*. Jones brought her round step by step, and it was when she was heading 010° that *Victory*'s MAYDAY came through. Radar had her too, mercifully only four miles to leeward, on *Windrose*'s starboard bow. It was 1134 and the signal was just audible.

Victory was scudding round the compass, out of control. Her yard slides had iced up and the mizzen and fore topsails could not be furled into the mast. Black ice had developed on the sails and her stability was going. Buckle was swearing, his voice identifiable, but *Windrose* was closing, however slowly, the radar echo appearing only on every fourth or fifth crest when *Victory* mounted the swell. By noon, the barometer was down to 27.40 and the wind a long moan: *like the end of the world*, thought Barnaby Jones.

At 1237, Bellew lost control. 'Can't hold her, sir!' he shouted. 'She's coming up.'

The engine-room warning monitor was glowing red.

'Hard a-starboard, Mister!' Jones yelled as he snatched the engine-room phone. He listened briefly then slammed it back into its rest. He watched the steering tape ticking steadily to port as the ship swung remorselessly to the northward. 'Dear God...' he muttered to himself.

There was nothing he could do. There was a *crack!* like an exploding mortar shell: the fore topmast staysail blew out in tatters.

There was an overwhelming roaring, like a flight of jets going through the sound barrier. The Captain jerked round to peer through the after window.

A black mountain range of ocean was galloping down towards his beautiful ship. When it struck, he could do nothing but shield his head from the shattering glass. The ship was listing, further over and further to her beam ends. He tried to haul himself up from what had been the deck. Through the bright rectangle which had been a window, he could see the yardarm of the main course dragging through the water. A line of foam frothed the length of *Windrose*'s lee rail, her scuppers threshing underwater from fo'c'sle to quarter. Another sea like this, and she would never rise again. He could do nothing now.

He could hear shouts from somewhere. She was slowly — God! so slowly — righting herself... Up she came, shaking herself like the grand lady she was, tons of water streaming from her upperworks and decks. Unbelievably, the container boxes and hatches had held. She was no lower in the water, but remained beam-on to the swell.

Jones pressed the port engine starter button again and again. The red light went out. There was a gentle, steady trembling, and then miraculously her head began to pay off. As she steadied to her course, two events followed each other in swift succession.

'Engine room — bridge,' croaked a voice at the other end of the phone. 'The Chief's bad, sir; burned in the roll. We're taking him to the bay.'

As Jones started to enquire further, the port lookout in the after end of the wheelhouse yelled at the top of his voice, 'Captain, sir! There she is...' The young seaman's face was white with fear. '*There*, sir... Oh, my God...' The man was mesmerized.

There, her lee rail awash while she floated up the same swell as *Windrose*, was *Techno Victory*. And as Captain Jones watched, the dynaship's foremast went, snapped like a twig. Her topsail thrashed, crumpled like a leaf against the tubular mast. Then, like ninepins in a bowling alley, her masts began to carry away, one after the other. What remained of her above the water, the squall forced over on its side. She wallowed, her twisted masts level with the boiling surface, her foremast and mainmast dragging along her side. In a moment her hull must be holed, speared by these globular spars. Of her officers and crew, there was no sign.

'Starboard twenty, Mr Karatz,' Jones rapped. 'There's nothing we can do for her but stand by.'

Techno Victory was sighted once again, drifting deep in the maelstrom while *Windrose* was swept to leeward. Captain Jones transmitted a sighting report at 1548, then concentrated on saving his own vessel.

At 1550, the sun was setting feebly to the westward and, as darkness shut in, the terrors of the gale seemed magnified: all became blackness and flying water, but at 1730 the wind moderated for ten minutes. The glass was reading 27.30 and *Windrose*'s ordeal was eased suddenly.

'Don't let up on your steering, Mr Bellew. We're going through the centre. Watch out for the wind on the other tack.'

And, true as his warning, the storm suddenly hurled itself upon them from the south. It swirled, circling swiftly before settling down again from the west. But scudding twice around the compass, *Windrose* remained watertight. An hour later, the barometer read 27.60; by eight bells, the guts had gone out of the wind. Captain Jones was able to call men on deck again to hoist the inner jib. *Windrose* ran, corkscrewing before the gale until she was north of Staten Island; then she rounded up and lay-to, the Falkland current carrying her safely northward until the storm's strength was dissipated by the tip of Patagonia. The barque was safe; leaving the Falklands close to the westward, she set course for Montevideo.

The ship was in a mess, but Barnaby allowed the exhausted hands to sleep until dawn broke again. And that evening, when the steward brought his captain a rum-laced mug of cocoa and a corned-beef sandwich, Sparks also appeared with the typed summary of the BBC news. The headlines hinted at The Horn catastrophe, but it was the city news at the end which caught Barnaby's eye: *The diminutive shipping company, OSC, has been bought out by the giant, Global Sea Transport.*

Windrose, her master and crew now belonged to Akroyd Stok.

Captain Barnaby Jones, Extra Master and veteran of the Falklands War, moved silently out to his glistening, slippery poop deck. Above him, the first stars were piercing through the flying scud. The waves were breaking regularly now, their crests phosphorescent in the darkness... A brace of Molly birds floated past, sheltering during the night from the wind. A white gull flashed by, its feathers bloodied from the reflection of the port light, then was gone.

'God,' he muttered bitterly. 'Why did You protect me, just to be taken over by Stok?' He returned to the wheelhouse and squared his shoulders: he would get in some sleep and feel better in the morning. Gavin had had the prescience to sign on Captain Jones officially for the voyage ... and no one, not even Stok, could legally break that contract, whatever else the swine was contemplating.

He turned to face for'd, where the white horses gleamed in the black seas into which the bows were now dipping regularly. With this current and a reasonably free wind, *Windrose* should make Montevideo in five days. There was time to think things out.

CHAPTER EIGHT: HOT SPOT

The teak of *Wandering Star*'s minuscule poop deck was so hot that Hannah Jones's sandalled feet could hardly bear the heat; and this despite the steady winds of the South-East Trades. She edged her deckchair another three feet towards that of the Nursing Sister, Jasmine Htut, to steal the growing patch of shade beginning to be cast by the mizzensail.

Wandering Star was bowling on a broad reach along the 50 north parallel. It was now 1410 on Tuesday, 16 July and Hannah could smell the sweet incense of land. It was an exhilarating moment after twenty-three days at sea. She closed her eyes and tried to sleep in the sweltering heat which persisted despite *Wandering Star*'s eighteen and a half knots.

Captain Staithe went sick on the eleventh day out from Wellington, just when Pitcairn had come up on their port bow. It was an evocative moment identifying the browny-green island from so far off, with its circle of cloud above, and fascinating to recall Captain Bligh and the *Bounty* legend. For over two hours Staithe, whose face and neck had yellowed during the week, had debated whether to hold on against the adverse July current, or to beat nor'-eastward for six days until *Wandering Star* crossed the Equator to reach the Equatorial Counter Current. Both the Second Mate, Burn Tinewood, and Hannah had advised taking the latter course between Oeno and Ducie Island, despite three days plugging against the southerly current pushing down from the Equator. *Wandering Star* had made good twelve knots, once the South-East Trades picked her up north-west of Easter Island.

Those were days of sailing Hannah would never forget: the great schooner listing to her lee rail, the seas hissing down her sides while she danced northward in happy abandonment. It was at the height of their enjoyment that the Weatherfax announced the hurricane-force gales against which the Horn ships were battling. The news was disturbing for her, when she compared *Wandering Star*'s idyllic conditions with those against which her father was fighting for his life. Only two hours ago the 'Daily State' had come through from the radio office, and the worst of their fears were confirmed.

Mina, the 16,400-ton Dutch Flettner, had been caught on the edge of the storm. A MAYDAY had been picked up by a HAM operator listening in New Zealand: apparently the tip of one tower had touched the seas during an excessive roll when her stabilizers had failed; she had wisely taken the Magellan Strait and would safely make Montevideo. The pride of the GST fleet, Akroyd Stok's dynaship, *Techno Victory*, had been overwhelmed. Four of her six masts had been carried away, but she had survived; the hull was being towed by a Dutch tug into Port Stanley. The helicopter services had been unable to cope in the hurricane-force winds but, because the crew had stayed with the floating hulk, only the men on deck had been casualties, crushed by the collapsing steel spars and then drowned. The night must have been a nightmare. Hannah thanked God that her father had brought his ship through without serious damage. And from her inner self, a whispered message of love flowed to her father: a surge of tenderness went out to him, and, as the urge to speak to him grew intense, her anxiety became more and more painful.

Siddartho Maru, the Japanese aerofoil ship, seemed to be retiring from the race, her two sails gone. And her rival, *Sherrilee*, in which Jason Mercer was a Race Observer, had had trouble with a jammed aerofoil. She too was repairing in Montevideo and hoped to be continuing the race. The dynaship monster, the two-masted Belgian *Dynasaur* had been seriously damaged and had limped into Port Stanley for jury repairs. *Pollux*, the German dynaship, had survived, having 'reefed' her sails in plenty of time: she ran under bare poles for the lee of the Falklands. Her fellow countryman, the horizontal windmill, *Amazone*, was not so lucky: she was lost without trace, no survivors, nothing.

Ocean Kite, the big Singaporean, had suffered damage and lost her airborne sails. The Portuguese vertical turbine, *Sao Isabel*, had patriotically and prudently opted for the Magellan Strait and taken shelter until the storms had blown themselves out; with her monster 'hoops', she was making for Uruguay. *Sea Falcon*, the American rival to *Wandering Star*, had hove-to under bare poles and though being knocked down to her beam-ends, she was making for Montevideo, as was *Stella Venus*. There *Yankee Flyer* awaited her, having reached port under power only after all her kites had blown away. The little Polish barque, *Wicker*, had survived, having got off her canvas in time; but she had taken a hammering and nearly foundered through flooding, one of her hatch covers smashed in by a monster sea. Three men had been swept over the side and lost. She was struggling to renew her sails in time for the start from Montevideo on Wednesday, 17 July.

Hannah could still not erase from her mind the images of the awful, sudden end of that modern and technically sound ship, the *Amazone*, disappearing without trace in the numbing waters of the Screaming Fifties. The sea, as always, was master, whatever man presumed. The rescue services had been overwhelmed and it was a miracle that so many survivors from the other ships had reached the Falklands, Chile and Terra del Fuego.

Captain George Staithe was very sick and Jasmine Htut, who had qualified in tropical diseases, was fairly certain that hepatitis was the cause of the man's illness. The Mate, the Portuguese, Joào Otaz, had assumed command and a radio signal had been sent to the British Consul at Colón. Rumours were rife, including the assertion that Akroyd Stok himself was on his way out by Concorde from England to take over the ship. If that happened, the seamen were muttering, they'd walk off in a body at the next port of call: Kingston, Jamaica, if Stok joined at Colón, at the eastern end of the canal. There'd be no time at Balboa, at the western end. Joào Otaz seemed as capable as the sarcastic Staithe, and certainly more jovial, so the *Star* ought to reach Balboa all right: the ETA for the landfall buoy and the pilot boat was 1600; only three quarters of an hour to go...

The schooner had passed three hundred miles north of the Galapagos, so had seen nothing of those unique islands. Her sounding transponders easily picked up the Cocos Ridge, and Hannah had used it to confirm the Satnav position yesterday; she was secretly feeling somewhat smug and pleased with herself, the doped Staithe having buttered her up in front of Burn Tinewood, the Navigator and Second Mate. Hannah despised him intensely: she wondered what Mrs Tinewood thought of her fancy-free husband. Both Jasmine Htut and Hannah were becoming bored with him: he was too pleased with himself and his hands were everywhere. She hated pawing men.

She glanced up as the lookout hailed from his covered crow's nest above the radar on the foremast. His outstretched arm pointed to the starboard bow and there, after so many interminable days, stretched an olive-green strip of low-lying coast shimmering in the heat.

A mirage danced on the horizon, the inverted and luscious, green forest trees jumbled, and tremulously shining among the matchbox images of the city towers of Balboa. Her heart leapt with pleasure. In a short time, she would be walking down the gangway for the first time in almost three weeks: what must it have been like in Anson's days, when months were spent on board without touching land? Did Nelson not have only two *hours* ashore in all his two-and-a-half *years* of blockading and chasing Villeneuve's fleet to the West Indies and back, bottling up the French off Toulon and pursuing Boney to Aboukir Bay?

Hannah woke Jasmine, picked up her straw mat, then walked aft to the ladder. She would take a shower and spruce herself up before manning the charthouse with Burn Tinewood. The pilot was scheduled to be picked up in fifty minutes' time.

Like a shroud, the night fell suddenly, bringing with it an oppressive airlessness. Hannah Jones stood for a moment by herself at the after end of *Wandering Star*'s poop deck. The ship slumbered, her sails lowered, her teak decks steaming as they dried from the scrubbing they had been given after the tugs' filthy hawsers had left their grimy imprints. Joào Otaz had formally been given temporary command by the ailing Staithe and the Portuguese was determined to start as he meant to carry on. *Wandering Star*, apart from rust patches around her catheads and midship gunwales, looked a useful, working thoroughbred; Hannah felt a pride in belonging to her as she leaned across the rail and gazed into the steamy night that bore down on Balboa.

The port served as Panama City's gate into the western end of the canal and, as such, was a haven for the human parasites living off the seafarers who, for a few hours, had money to spend in Balboa. Colón, at the far end of the canal, and Balboa, provided all that seamen wanted, hungry as they were for the bright lights; but, Burn Tinewood had told her, this was a cosmopolitan sewer with little charm, so different from the East where magic still lurked.

True to self! Hannah thought. Burn was painting things as he saw them. He knew it all, pompous ass! He was an excellent navigator, but why did he have to spoil things? He might be trying to put her off going ashore, but nothing would stop her seeing for herself what the bright lights offered...

The tugs had nudged *Wandering Star* alongside Number Sixteen jetty, where she now lay stern-to with *Storm Petrel*, the Australian schooner who had beaten them all by two days. Hannah could see the high tips of *Techno Phanta*'s vertical windmill blades soaring above the container cranes. She had identified *Niger*, when the *Star* had entered at dusk. The Liquid Nitrogen Gas carrier looked like a bloated whale where she lay at her buoy three miles off-shore, her two Walker Wingsail aerofoils swinging free to the evening puffs. The pilot said nothing, but had nodded his unshaven, blue-stubbled face towards her and spat over the side. He resented having to take that sort of cargo through 'his' canal: the day was not far off now, he reminded all and sundry, when Panamanians could decide for themselves what ships they would allow to use their canal.

Hannah could spot also the tall, twin towers of *Jacques-Yves Cousteau*, the Flettner *éolienne* in the next basin and, further out in the harbour, the grotesque silhouette of *Red Star* at anchor, the outline of her two dynamasts and triangular fore-and-aft sails picked out with glowing strings of electric lights: the Russians were not missing a trick. Then she heard the distant thumping of a band blaring its raucous rumba from somewhere near the dock gate. Her blood quickened and she smiled to herself: a timely break! A sense of adventure gripped her.

She wanted to know this place, hear its music, follow the tempo of a South American night, smell the spices, let go, have a good old party! Jasmine would come too, surely? The thought of changing from her sensible cotton slacks into a full-skirted dress suddenly appealed: she wore any clothes with confidence. She pouted out her lower lip and blew at the drop of perspiration dripping from her nose.

The party assembled to go ashore, with Hannah in her colourful, mosaic-pattern flowing dress. She felt great, as they all did. Burn knew just the place, and he'd look after them. *Oh, yes…! And pester me too, the mood he's in*, thought Hannah. But getting ashore was exciting in itself.

El Draco, one of the local clubs, was the rendezvous for the stream of transiting voyagers. 'Suitable for us,' Burn volunteered.

The first drink always flows deliciously up to the brain. The fun begins while the glasses are topped up. Burn's eyes, while he drew on his Havana , roved around the place with a proprietary pride, but always steered back to Hannah. Couples were swaying to a samba in the centre of the low, palm-festooned room. The usual band was thumping out the rhythm: they were a seedy-looking lot in some sort of feathered outfit, garish and brightly coloured. Burn flicked his cigar towards the floor. 'The cabaret next,' he grinned. 'Ever seen a South American one?' They started joking, the strong, spicy punch sending Hannah's blood coursing. Jasmine had not turned up yet.

Burn went on, glancing sideways at Hannah in that ridiculous, suave fashion of his which was getting sorely on Hannah's nerves. 'Drake played hell on the other side of the Isthmus. His sailors chased the nuns off the cliff of La Popa, a hill behind Cartagena, forty years after the Spaniards built the fortress. No wonder they called him "El Draco". He's buried in Nombre de Dios Bay. Did you know that, sweetie?' Burn held his hand out to her across the table. She ignored it but, when the band stopped, the lights dimming, he muttered something inaudible and came to sit beside her on a cane stool.

'What d'you say?' she asked.

'In his hammock,' Burn whispered and, cupping his hand to his ear, he leaned towards her, adding facetiously in a West Country burr, 'Cap'n, art tha' sleepin' there below?'

Mounting exasperation diluted Hannah's early cheerfulness. *Why do middle-aged men so often overact the charm?* she thought. There were two of them on board: the Captain and Burn. Both married. The thought revived her irritation as the image of Jason Mercer's face flashed through her mind. Why hadn't he got in touch in Wellington? Too reserved, like her Dad... Of a saturnine nature... Men were never where you wanted them to be, damn it... Some didn't know when to stop, like Burn; some, when to start. Or how... Hannah could no longer hear the noises around her, her thoughts miles away as she sat in the high-backed cane chair, a trim figure holding a glass which she stroked rhythmically.

She had missed her father when she was a child. He apparently had never guessed her expectant dreams, having dismissed his long absences with a hearty hug and an expensive present from abroad. He talked only about his blessed ship, her new rigging, the canvas sails … but he'd never noticed that her own cotton skirts were getting longer. Then he would be off again. Holding his daughter firmly in his arms, each time he would look deeply into her eyes. 'I know, Hannah,' he would say, 'that I shall always be proud of you!' A momentary tenderness in his eyes, a pause … and then he'd be gone. She would return to her studies. 'Yes, Dad. Of course, Dad.'

With whom now to share her own love of life, her love of the sea, its poetry and tangible reality? And Hannah knew she was carrying out a sterile exercise which, like underdeveloped negatives, left no prints in the memory album.

Her eyes were fixed on the green plant near the musicians, but slowly she began to register the movements around her. 'What's going on?' she asked abruptly. 'Where's Jasmine?'

'Don't worry,' Burn said, his eyes devouring this delicious girl with those shapely legs. 'Something's happened to the Old Man, I expect. She was trying to fix hospital for him.'

She knew that he had been regarding her for a while, and now she sensed that he was watching her avidly. She could read his mind as he worked out what ploy to use for getting round her; she guessed he realized that, tantalizing though she might be, she was nevertheless a tough, self-possessed seawoman. She was sure that he could not fathom the source of her strength, and certain, also, that he wanted her and found the chase as exciting as playing a marlin. His voice was too loud when he announced, 'Let's get high! Life's too short.' He drained his glass and ostentatiously summoned a waiter to order another round.

She felt the insidious effect of the alcohol and of the humid heat, as she listened to the lilting beat of the latest 'coco' which began to pervade the room. The glowing lamps dimmed one by one to leave two cones of blue light focused in a circle at the end of the room. The music faded but after a moment started pulsating again. The spotlight changed slowly to violet, to orange and then suddenly flicked out, leaving them in darkness.

Hannah could feel the excitement, sense the expectation at the tables around her as she herself was caught up in it. A searing light-beam flooded the centre of the floor... A sigh floated around the room as the silver-sheathed woman stood motionless in the spot. She was red-lipped, heavy-lidded: the traditional cabaret dancer, the woman of men's dreams, or so the management judged. Hannah's heart, too, started throbbing a little faster.

The music started, the rhythm slowly working to a crescendo, doing its work. The woman barely moved at first, her hands only suggesting the bewitching music as her palms slid along her thighs. Then she emphasized, with unimaginable suppleness, each beat of the music as she offered every angle of her body for their titillation.

It was soon obvious that the locals were acting as cheerleaders, for the whole audience began swaying to the music. And as the artiste gradually went through the traditional sequences, Hannah began to peer about her in the darkness, fascinated by the reactions of the throng, a motley from all corners of the globe. Tourists, passers-in-the-night, seamen, all were here, mostly with women, and laughing brazenly while they knocked back their fizzy beers at five dollars a glass.

At first, there had been the obvious wise-cracking from those who had dined too well. But now there was silence as the woman appeared in and out of the fading lights, the contours of her shapely body exaggerated by the slits in the silver lamé which still draped her thighs. Gasps of anticipation breathed around the room, even from this sophisticated and worldly lot.

Each time another shimmering trifle slithered to the floor, Hannah wanted to laugh. An unbridled lust was beginning to pervade the room and she glanced at her companions. The dim rose light was reflected in Burn's face, which was a study: his dark eyes gleamed excitedly, even in this subdued atmosphere. He was as still as a statue, but the tip of his tongue licked his thin lower lip. And as the roll of the samba drums pounded to a frenzy, all the lights concentrated on the provocative woman standing there, her fingers on the tags of her last piece of shiny satin. She stood astride, contemptuous of them, proud, almost spitting...

The lights flicked out. There was a flash of dusky beauty. Then, total darkness... The silence was finally broken by a husky sigh around the room. The lights flicked on again, the beam concentrating on the crumpled silver gown in the centre of the pool of light. As the shout of applause exploded about her, Hannah was shaken by uncontrollable laughter. She had been sipping the drinks mechanically and the thought shot through her mind: why didn't they have a male stripper as well? That would cause Burn to chew his glowing cigar! How pathetic it all was. Watching the crowd of drooling slobs who had not the wit to make their own fun, she knew that she was bored and had drunk enough.

'Oh, let's go!' she said impulsively. Burn jumped up, winking to the others. *If he thinks he's in luck...* Hannah halted. 'Don't bother, I'll take a taxi.'

But Burn was pushing her between the tables, towards the door and out on to the pavement. He put his arm around her shoulders, but Hannah shook herself free. Then the warm hand was gripping her shoulder again. 'Look at me, Hannah, damn you...'

Hannah turned to look into his smouldering, dark eyes. 'Leave me alone, Burn.' Her steely voice chopped each word slowly.

But, confused and unable to realize that he had created this inane confrontation, Burn's drunken desire flamed. He started wheedling. 'Come on, sweetie, I know what you want…'

The speed and strength of her double slap to his face could not have been premeditated: her ring sliced Burn's right cheek, which swiftly oozed with pearls of blood. He stepped back. 'You, you cow! I'll get you … and your father. I'll … I'll drink to that right now!' With a defiant snort, Burn stumbled back into the El Draco.

Hannah's hand was burning and for a moment, she was disconcerted by the turn of events; she could not take her eyes off her sole valuable possession, a large burnt topaz held by four thick claws of gold, a present from her father. Hannah stood still, conspicuous on the crowded pavement, until a taxi stopped alongside her. '*Señora?*'

Feeling utterly alone, Hannah reached for the car door. She leaned back and said wearily to the driver: '*Al puerto, dique numero diez y seis.*' The sound of her own voice still surprised her. During the ride back to the docks, her eyes took in the endless neon displays and multi-coloured illuminations. She had wanted to see the bright lights, hadn't she?

The sight of *Wandering Star*, the warm, foetid air, the lingering muzziness of the potent drinks made her feel elated. Giggling quietly while she clambered up the length of the brow, she burst suddenly into song:

'From anywhere
To anywhere,
Blow the wind, blow… Blow … the … wind, BLOW!'

Stepping on to the deck, she smiled at the perplexed sailor at the head of the gangway. 'Still sailing at seven?' she asked.

'Aye, Miss, calling the hands at 0600.'

There were two messages for her in her cabin:

The mate is the new skipper now. Captain Staithe is in hospital.
JASMINE

There was no signature to the second message:

Received by telephone 2107:
Get in touch with the British Consul in Colón.

She slipped from her clothes. Flicking out the light, she lay naked on the bed, the air of the punkah-louvre blowing the length of her body. Transiting the canal, tomorrow would be a long day and she would be on the bridge for most of it. Burn would be useless on the morning after...

CHAPTER NINE: SOLITARY PLAYER; LONELY UNCERTAINTY

Dawn on the Equator, Hannah was certain, was the loveliest moment in the interminable day. If she could live in these latitudes, she would laze about forever.

While she waited by herself on the bridge for *Wandering Star*'s temporary captain to appear, she watched the port of Balboa gradually awakening for the new day: Wednesday, 17 July, and the *Star*'s transit of the Panama Canal. Awed as always, she watched the sun leaping upwards from the grey-green hills behind the city. It was 0630 and the tugs were securing alongside at bow and stern. Joào Otaz, his blue jowls freshly shaved, his gleaming smile jerking his bridge team and the somnambulant pilot to reluctant wakefulness, planted himself in the middle of his bridge. He nodded at the pilot. The warps, their ratguards removed, splashed into the filthy water. *Wandering Star* was at last starting her transit of the canal, though deckhands were adrift.

'Jack and Pedro,' the Bo'sun reported. 'Drunk. Wouldn't jump ship; not in this dump, Skipper.'

'Get a message to the Consul here,' Joào nodded at the ship's Race Observer, Señor Fratelli, the surprisingly taciturn Italian who had kept himself to himself for the whole voyage. 'Ask the Port RO to fly the men up to Colón,' Joào Otaz ordered. 'I'll need 'em on the other side.'

At 0700, the schooner was lying off the Miraflores Lock, the lowest of the three locks which raised the water level eighty feet from the Pacific to the Atlantic — and Hannah still marvelled at the intricate movement of the planets. (Why didn't the Atlantic run round the Horn to equalize the levels?) *Wandering Star* had to wait twenty minutes before being squeezed into the lock alongside *Jacques-Yves Cousteau*, the French *éolienne*, an advanced Flettner-type ship. The canal workers did not have their tickets 'punched' until the Miraflores clock jangled its seven strokes. By the time the silent, electrically powered 'mules' were manned and ready to handle the first ship, it was 0728. The lock gates slid shut astern of the *Star*'s shapely counter; the sluices were opened and the Pacific sea water deluged into Miraflores Lock.

Hannah had never before experienced a large lock, so was amazed by the speed at which the two ships climbed up the greasy, filthy walls. Surging ahead towards the end gate and lunging against their springs in the swirling water, the ships were held in check, then controlled adroitly by the 'mules': these buff-coloured diesel tractors looked like beavering cockroaches, thought Hannah. The flooding eased as the levels balanced; the end gate slid open and *Jacques-Yves Cousteau* steered out of the lock under her own power. *Wandering Star* followed, the pilot keeping closely in the Frenchman's wake, which led across the lakelet of Pedro Miquel. The water level in Gatun Lake was sustained by this vital lock gate at Port Miquel which, like the other lock gates, was protected from rogue ships by massive chain cables: a 10,000-ton ship moving at four knots could be brought to rest within seventy feet. Both ships were locked into Pedro Miquel by 0810, where they were lifted the extra twenty-five feet up to the level of the Gatun Lake, the sheet of water which had to be reached by negotiating the narrow and impressive Culebra Cut.

Hannah listened to the garrulous Panamanian pilot who, while talking to Joào Otaz and conning the ship through The

Cut, was proudly proclaiming how the Panama Canal came to be built. As she listened, she was overawed by the savage scenery which crowded upon them: the jagged, yellow rocks which, overhanging the ship's mastheads, were so close that they seemed to scrape the trucks.

Hannah was depressed by the contrast between this primaeval jungle and the 'civilization' represented by Balboa.

The equatorial jungle was poised to engulf the planet again should Man destroy himself. These rampant trees with their fleshy, rubbery leaves; the muddy-green water, teeming with life and the bacteria which had decimated through yellow fever 160,000 of the original toilers who had hacked out this amazing canal. The awesome power of nature was reducing the crew to silence as they watched their ship gliding between these savage cliffs.

The end of the Culebra Cut was opening up a mile ahead, where another collection of islands appeared to block the channel into the large Gatun Lake. Fascinated, Hannah listened to the pilot who was warming to his description of *his* canal.

Since Christopher Columbus first set eyes on the Pacific, Man had dreamed of his ships reaching the great ocean through the Isthmus, of navigating between Europe and Eastern Asia without beating against fierce contrary winds round the dreaded Cape Horn. As long ago as 1550, the Portuguese navigator, Antonio Galvas, had suggested that a 130-mile canal could be cut either through the Isthmus of Ticuantepe; through Nicaragua or Panama; or by starting from the Gulf of Darien, which was a cut of only eighty miles. European wars and riots in America rendered all schemes impractical; it was not until 1879 that Ferdinand de Lesseps' dream was seriously considered as being practical. For ten million francs the French nation bought, through the Wyse Concession, the right to begin work and the first Panama Company was formed.

de Lesseps' plan, which was based upon the sea-level principle, would cost 658 million francs and take eight years to build. The canal would follow the railway route, but the railroad company's agreement was not guaranteed. The combined difficulties of controlling the territorial waters of the Chagres River on the Atlantic side; of raising the cash; and digging the enormous cut at Culebra eventually sank the first scheme.

'That's the Gatun Lake,' the pilot called out, pointing towards the steamy, grey sheet of water opening up ahead. 'It's fed by the Chagres; the level's controlled by the dam at Gatun, alongside the lock: the dam's the key to the whole complex. Put it out of action and there's no canal.' He grinned as a brace of US helicopters, guns visible but covered, swept inquisitively over the schooner. 'Take her down the channel, Captain. Between the buoys. Follow *Cousteau*. And I'll finish my story…'

In 1894 the French government created a second Panama Company; during the first year of the new century and through de Lesseps' far-sighted medical policy (the labourers were immunized against yellow fever), five million cubic yards of soil had been shovelled away. Then, when the United States again came on the scene, the French once more ran into trouble.

The Americans were determined to own the Panama Canal. The Californian gold rush was in full spate, and transport was saturated. It was a national duty for Americans and especially for Northern Yankees, to control their communications: should Europeans own the canal, the United States could be cut off from their South American interests. As early as 1876, three years before de Lesseps' original scheme, a movement took hold in America to start building a canal through Nicaragua. Preliminary work began but stopped when a fresh investigation of the project was instituted: big money had already been spent in a foreign country and on a project which, when finished, would not belong to the USA.

A dispute was engineered by the Americans with Mexico. Insisting that the isthmus had to be kept open, the States bought the five-mile strip of land on either side of the present canal. The price was forty million dollars; the rent, a quarter of a million dollars for the next ninety-nine years. Thirty years later, the USA was making four million dollars a *month* from canal dues. 'They started work in 1906,' the Balboa pilot concluded, 'but they adopted the lock system.' He pointed across the port bow: 'There's that Gatun dam which controls the whole thing: over seven thousand feet long, two thousand wide at its base and it rises one hundred and fifteen feet above the Pacific sea level.' He sucked his metal-filled teeth when the chopper flew in again, closing from the westward. 'Submarines, army, air force … the lot.'

Ships were now sliding past in the channel, Pacific-bound. Speed was restricted to fifteen knots and it was not until 1035 that *Wandering Star* and *Jacques-Yves Cousteau* were secured in Gatun's first lock. The ship was entering the second, final lock at 1120 when the Captain, seeing that Burn Tinewood was now *compos mentis* at the chart table, told Hannah she could leave the bridge to get herself a cool drink. It was swelteringly hot and she was thankful to go aft for a breather. She found Jasmine Htut and, together, they idly watched the last formalities taking place over the ship's side. Mail was passed, papers signed and at last the lock gate was opened. *Wandering Star* forged ahead and within minutes, having dropped her ebullient pilot, was letting go her anchor in the grey waters of Cristóbal Bay, Colón's anchorage behind the breakwaters. A boat was already on its way from the port, so she'd be ashore soon to pick up her letter at the consul's office. Collecting her bag and passport from her cabin, Hannah hastened back to the bridge. Joào Otaz seemed unusually morose where he leaned across the wing to watch the launch lolloping through the dirty waters. He turned when he heard his Assistant Navigator pattering on the burning deck behind him.

'May I go ashore for my letter, sir?' she asked. 'I can take that boat.' Instead of the usual smile, she received only a grunt.

'You'll have to ask your new Captain.' He jerked his head towards the approaching boat. 'Captain Randy Buckle, Extra Master Mariner, *señorita*, at your service,' and he mumbled under his breath.

'Sorry, sir. What did you say?'

'Old Spanish proverb,' he said. 'I'm not sure —' he glared at the boat turning to come alongside — 'that I still believe in it.' His sonorous voice rolled out the words: '*Siempre cree en Dios quien cruza el Océano*'. He looked quizzically at her. 'Who so crosses the Ocean, always believes in God.' Shaking his head, he strode to the ladder to greet *Wandering Star*'s new captain. If ever anyone could suggest contempt in the way he walked, Joào Otaz was that man. Burn Tinewood came up quietly behind her to watch the red-bearded giant clambering from the bumboat.

'Providence works in mysterious ways, Miss Jones,' he murmured sarcastically. 'Randy survives the *Victory* disaster while most of his crew drowns. He's been flown up from Port Stanley by Akroyd Stok, bless his cotton socks. Buckle may be a bloody good seaman, but I don't trust him further than I could heave our anchor.' Tinewood moved to the side to watch the sweating man in the tropical fawn suit scrambling up the ladder. 'You may not think much of me, Miss Jones, but you'll positively adore me after a spell with that bloke... Anything goes, provided you like him. *Yuk*! A high-tech skipper in our high-tech ship: makes me sick.' The Second Mate took himself off below.

João was trying to cut off a respectful salute. Buckle stepped on board, glanced fore and aft, then roared, 'Well, me boyos! You can weigh that bloody hook.' He glared at Otaz. 'You heard me, Mister Mate? Weigh anchor. We're going to win this effing race. Kingston, here we come...' He flung down his grip for the Bo'sun's Mate to collect. 'Get all hands on deck. I'm setting full sail.'

Hannah stood back as he rolled past, stinking of rum and cigars. The hands were already being piped and she could hear the running feet. She would wait until the ship was clear, then persuade Sparks to signal the consul to relay her letter to Jamaica. A plane would reach Kingston before the ship, for it was a two-and-a-half-day passage for the schooner. But, as she went below to shift into her sea-going gear, she remained silent, uneasy. Something, she sensed, was going very wrong.

CHAPTER TEN: LA PLATA

Jason could hardly believe that the ordeal was almost over: in two hours' time, *Sherrilee* would be securing in the outer basin of the great port of Montevideo. Captain Klosson and his Exec had done all they could to 'chamfer up' the ship's appearance after the battering she had suffered, but however much the paint brush had been used to cover the rust, nothing could conceal the fore aerofoil which, despite the Chief's tireless efforts, had persisted in remaining locked on a bearing of Green 80°. The absurdity did not diminish Klosson's irascibility.

Punta del Este and Punta Negra were slipping astern on the starboard quarter and Klosson's pilot request had been acknowledged on Port Wave. The hands were clearing away the pilot ladder on the starboard side and at any moment the launch should be sighted to the northward off the lightship which protected English Bank. When Arquímedes Bank bore due south, *Sherrilee* would alter to the north to pick up the entrance channel into the port of Montevideo and its docks. The air was heavy and mist trailed over the brown-green waters of the Plate.

The low-lying, olive-green coast stretched westwards to the city where *Sherrilee* would be spending the next three days; even if the yard could take her in hand, the Chief doubted whether the Uruguayans possessed the precision equipment to machine the main bearing ring. But Klosson swore that, even if the yard could only free the vanes and set them amidships, *Sherrilee* would be among the starters on Tuesday, 16 July.

Today was Sunday, 14 July, and nothing could be done: Uruguayan dockies behaved much as their European counterparts. The ship was turning north for English Bank and the pilot boat. This South American spring was surprisingly cold: a chill northerly wind was blowing straight off the Brazilian Serra de Paranapiacaba and across the humid swamps of the Paraná River. Rain could not be far off: Jason shivered and went down to his cabin for a sweater. He would have time to complete his log before returning to the bridge for the final approach to Montevideo.

'Well, Jason,' Franklin Dicker muttered behind him, 'I hope, for your sake, you'll have a less hairy trip on your next lap to Rio. D'you know yet what ship you've got?'

Jason shook his head. 'As soon as I can get ashore, I'm going round to the RO's office.'

They were watching the buoys coming up while the bay of Montevideo opened up ahead. Like every modern city around the world, a screen of concrete tower blocks lined the sandy beach from one side of the turquoise bay to the other. At the western end, Jason could see the breakwater and the entrance to the commercial port of Port Lobas.

'Looks good,' Franklin grinned. 'Anywhere would, after The Horn.' He pointed to a buoy they were leaving to port. 'I hoped you'd point it out to me, Jason. My father used to tell me that if three British cruisers could force a German pocket battleship to scuttle, it was worth America backing England after France collapsed.'

'It's a long time ago,' Jason said, '16 December 1939. *Graf Spee* was loose and raiding in the Atlantic.' He grinned. 'I've found a book on the battle in the ship's library.'

'Why did she scuttle?'

'Captain Langsdorff was ashamed at Hitler's order not to come out and fight again; once *Graf Spee* had taken shelter in Uruguayan neutral waters, HMS *Exeter*, *Ajax*, and the New Zealander, *Achilles*, were waiting for her, battered though they were after the battle. It was a cliff-hanger, with the whole world listening.'

'Tell me a bit more,' Franklin said, his eyes on the distant green wreck buoy. 'What about the battle itself?'

'It's become an historical example of tactical brilliance on the Royal Navy's part: three cruisers taking on a battleship.'

'*Graf Spee* was a battleship?' Franklin asked.

'A "pocket" battleship: Hitler built them, the first all-welded warships to keep down the weight; and with diesel engines, to get round the Allies' Treaty of London which forbade the Germans building warships of over 10,000 tons. *Graf Spee* had six eleven-inch guns in two triple turrets.' Jason added, 'The ideal commerce raider.'

'And the British?'

'*Exeter* had six eight-inch in three turrets; *Ajax* and *Achilles*, eight six-inch in four turrets. We fired torpedo salvoes twice during the battle, moves which apparently influenced Captain Langsdorff immensely. *Graf Spee* was hit by three of *Exeter*'s shells and over a dozen of the light cruisers' six-inch, so Langsdorff steamed into Montevideo and claimed neutrality privileges to repair his ship.'

'So why,' Franklin asked, 'did he blow up his ship?'

'The British were concentrating forces from all over the Atlantic — or so Langsdorff was led to believe. He scuttled *Graf Spee* because he did not want her radar to fall into our hands: he thought he had no chance. He committed suicide.'

'A sad story.'

'It was the first good news of the war for us,' Jason said. 'Langsdorff was found shot in his hotel room, in full uniform and lying across his ship's ensign.'

They were both silent as the green wreck buoy slid past. *Graf Spee*'s tomb meant nothing now to most people, but seventy-three officers and men of the Royal Navy and thirty-six German sailors had been killed. *Exeter*, the eight-inch cruiser who had drawn most of the fire, retired to the Falklands to be patched up before sailing back to Plymouth to be rebuilt. Three years later, in a gallant and hopeless battle in the Java Sea, she, with a mixed bag of Allied light units, was blown out of the water by an overwhelming force of Japanese cruisers and aircraft. The survivors who were picked up spent the rest of their hellish war in Japanese prison camps.

To Jason, watching the green buoy bobbing rhythmically in the River Plate's slop, the theatrical drama of films like *Bridge on the River Kwai* seemed inappropriate but he could not analyse why he felt thus. When watching television productions of those days so long ago, he often felt angry at the stereotyped caricatures served up to fuel ill-founded prejudices. What *could* they know of the context of the times and how men *really* felt? It was too puerile to decry those servicemen's inner feelings, to assert that they fought only because they were ordered to do so; to suggest that idiots at the top and our politicians were responsible for the catalogue of defeats and reverses which they suffered.

The truth is that those men were like us, thought Jason. *Is not the attitude of the 1930 pacifists analogous to what is going on today? We still harbour traitors within our land, the wreckers who with cynical contempt are destroying our society, for which those millions were willing to die half a century ago...* Jason turned slowly as the siren sounded above him, jerking him back to reality.

A pair of dumpy tugs were creaming through the fuscous water towards *Sherrilee*, their grubby sides festooned with old tyres and oil-saturated rope fenders. The harbour entrance was opening up, and Jason could see the tall masts of the barques and dynaships who were already anchored in the outer harbour.

There were the unmistakable, twin tall masts of the Belgian *Dynasaur*, dwarfing those of *Windrose*, who was anchored close to her. As *Sherrilee*, who was the last to reach Montevideo, eased to starboard, Jason began ticking off the names of the ships against the list stuck up on the Perspex board.

Ocean Kite, with a damaged winch; *Stella Venus* with her ducted fan out of action. *Sao Isabel*, with her two grotesque wind hoops, and the schooner, *Sea Falcon*, were alongside the long jetty at the entrance. On the big-ship berths further inside, their tophamper bemingled with the jumble of spars from ships from all over the world, were the larger competitors, the 28,000-ton kite ship, *Yankee Flyer*, and *Pollux*, the four-masted dynaship with her monster sails. These were all berthed head-to-tail along the discharging wharf where the cranes lay idle, their jibs pointing skywards on this Sunday, 14 July. The church bells were tolling, their sonorous clanging reverberating across the water to summon the faithful to Mass and to mourn the loss of *Amazone*. This R.F.A. horizontal windmill had vanished without trace, the tips of her blades presumably catching the crests of the huge seas off The Horn.

Tucked in a corner berth by herself was the unwieldy *Rêve de l'Avenir*, an arresting sight at sea but an embarrassment in harbour with her wide beam. And as the pilot checked *Sherrilee*'s way to enter 16 Dock, Jason spotted *Wicher*, the neat Polish barque, and the passenger cruise clipper, *Reina de la Mar*. Ahead of them on the repair wharves, where *Sherrilee* was heading, were the ships who had been damaged: *Dynasaur*, *Mina*, the Flettner, who without stabilizers had made it safely from the Magellan Strait, and, on the berth opposite, the giant *Siddartho Maru*, who had retired, with one of her aerofoil sails crumpled halfway along the leach.

Montevideo had been chosen by the SACOR committee as the first port of call instead of Rio de Janeiro because of its reasonable ship-repair rates and for its considerable facilities. But when the work would begin tomorrow, the yards would be stretched to have the casualties seaworthy again by next Wednesday, 17 July, for the controlled start to Rio. By all accounts, there had been a free-for-all among the shipping agents, a struggle which included blatant bribery to secure the repair yards. Each ship had, in addition, to complete her 'discharge-and-loading' requirements before being accepted for the controlled start: four boxes 'out' and seven 'in', to make things awkward.

Because there were insufficient container cranes to cater for everyone during these four days, each ship was being tested on her own cargo-handling gear. The all-up maximum weight of a 40-foot dry van was 30.4 tons, so ships like *Wicher* and *Windrose* had been designed to have their own crane arrangements. Each RO had to time the unloading and loading, so whether Jason could time *Sherrilee*'s evolution or not depended upon when the repairs to her for'd mast were completed. Though it was Sunday and the port was officially closed, *Sherrilee*'s agent had contrived to procure an army of repairmen to attack the ship the moment she secured on 16 Wharf. Jason was glad to bid his farewells and to slip with his gear over the brow while the ship's officers coped with the frenzy of preparing *Sherrilee* for the 'off' on the seventeenth.

The RO's office was near the dockyard main gate. Jason collected his mail, which was waiting in his pigeon-hole in the grubby office. The SRO was out when Jason looked in, but the ship appointments were pinned on the notice board: *J. Mercer to join* Rêve de l'Avenir *on Tuesday, 16 July* — the day on which the ROS exchanged ships. And in the pale sunlight outside the office, by the entrance to the main gate of Port Lobas, he finally read the last letter in his bundle of correspondence. The back of the buff envelope was sealed with a tab of Sellotape, the address was typewritten, marked 'by hand' and unstamped. The message inside was also typed:

To: Race Observer Mercer
From: Captain Jones
Meet me at the Carrasco Hotel 1800 onwards today, Sunday.
  Do not acknowledge.
  0820 14 July.

Jason looked up from the note he held in his hand. The fear which had dogged him in Wellington was beginning to ensnare him again, like the miasmatic mists over a marsh. Damn Barnaby Jones and his problems: Jason crumpled the note and strode down the bustling roadway towards the corner where the big French trimaran was berthed. He would take a look at her, then walk into the city before trying to find the Carrasco Hotel.

It was good to feel *terra firma* beneath one's feet again. Having dumped his gear in the SRO's office, Jason walked past red-roofed and gaily shuttered houses; the suburb bordered the stately buildings which, bequeathed by Spanish *conquistadores* and sturdy Portuguese navigators, constituted Montevideo's heart. Much of the city had been rebuilt in the late sixties, and already the modern tower blocks in the Plaza Independencia, the Edificio Ciudadela, looked shop-soiled compared with the substantial stone masonry of the older buildings, such as the massive pillared and arched gateway of the Ciudadela Fortress built in 1771, only three years before the Lexington incident and before George Washington's leadership triggered the American War of Independence.

The backbone of the city was the Avenue 18 de Julio, a broad tree-lined avenue leading from the impressive Independence Plaza at the seaward end. Here was honoured Uruguay's liberator and the father of the Uruguayan republic: tricorn in hand and seated squarely upon his sturdy mount, José Gervasio Artigas, his back to the Ciudadela, faced the parliamentary buildings which were his monument.

Jason dallied over lunch in a bar-restaurant in the dingy Juan Carlos Gomez cross-street running up from the port to the avenue of 18 Julio. The 'El Carioca' was a spit-and-sawdust joint, but the food was good; and Jason, watching the world go by, found it all a rare pleasure. He finished his lunch with a brandy and, stunning the blue-chinned waiter with a mammoth tip, he wrapped his anorak about him and stepped out into the chill afternoon for his rendezvous with Barnaby Jones.

By the time he reached the Plaza del Entrevero, he felt drowsy enough to flake out on the low wall encircling the spacious plaza with its central water monument. There, with the spikes of the palm leaves rustling above him, he fell asleep until awoken by the chill of the stone. The hubbub of the traffic and the cries of children playing around the pool brought him to his senses. Crossing to the avenue, he hailed a cab: he had seen enough of this once-beautiful city, which was becoming shabby. In comparison, the Carrasco Hotel was an imposing, restored Edwardian edifice with its tower, domed entrance and pillared, balanced wings. Palm trees leaned to the breeze wafting in from the Southern Atlantic, while the sun dipped towards the mouth of the Plate.

Sunk in an armchair in the foyer of the hotel, Captain Barnaby Jones was puffing at a Havana Havana. The sight of this avuncular Englishman cheered Jason: here was a man who would not allow the world to vanquish him. The habits of a lifetime took priority. The Captain climbed to his feet and pressed the service bell.

'The sun's over the yard-arm, Mercer: whisky?'

Jason, ensconced in the deep sofa, glanced through the large window to the luxuriant golf-course stretching down to the seashore. The whisky did its work: Jason got on naturally with the Captain, and in minutes they were swapping experiences of the first leg of SACOR. It was during the exorbitantly expensive and mediocre dinner that Barnaby came to the point.

'You know I still have no relief for James Mirson? No First Mate.'

'I imagined you'd have trouble, sir. We're a long way from home.'

There was a hardness in the Captain's eye which Jason had never seen before. Barnaby rose from the table and led the way to the lounge. 'Have you seen the Satnews? Are you keeping up with the city news?' Barnaby sipped his coffee, tapped the ash from his cigar.

Jason smiled and shook his head. 'The city's a different world from that of a Race Observer.'

'You know that Global has gobbled up my company, don't you? Stok has bought out OSC. He now has a total monopoly of the British square-riggers.'

Jason could not believe that Stok had the lot. 'What's he trying to achieve?'

'He's trying to sack me, so that he can appoint his own master and so make certain of *Windrose* losing the race. Then he can settle for his world motor fleet to continue: Global Sea Transport will then set the scene for the next generation of ships. They won't be sail-assisted if Stok has anything to do with it.'

Jason peered at the determined face gazing towards the darkening ocean. 'What are you going to do, Captain?'

'Stay in command, of course.'

'How can you, if Stok is the boss?'

A smile twitched at the corners of Jones's mouth. 'Gavin McBinney, my partner, beat him at his own game. Our OSC doesn't own *Windrose*. Before we signed on for the race, Gavin organized the sale of *Windrose* to a new company which we formed.'

'Its name?'

'McBinney and Jones. We're the sole owners.'

'And Stok's lawyers failed to bowl you out?'

Barnaby nodded. 'In the haste, his experts failed in their search to spot the transaction.' The Captain pressed the bell above his head and ordered, '*Dos portos ... gracias*.' Jones continued, 'She's still *our* ship, Jason, though Global now hires and operates us.'

'Stok can appoint his crews, presumably, if he's paying the wages?'

Jones's face hardened. 'That's the rub: he's got me over a barrel now that I have no First Mate. I've rated up the Bo'sun temporarily to Third Mate, until Gavin sends me out a dependable officer. Take a look at this...' He extracted a telex from his breast pocket:

From: Managing Director, Global Sea Transport
To: Master, Ship Windrose
Date: 13 July
Message: Mr Karl Karatz appointed First Mate Windrose and will join at Rio de Janeiro. All future crew will be signed on by agents of Global Sea Transport. Captain Jones's appointment will be reviewed on arrival UK. Acknowledge.
    STOK.

Jason sensed Barnaby watching him. 'But you've got Ben Bellew as Mate?'

'Temporary only. The Bo'sun, Tom Hawkins, would have made a better First. But I'll have to reduce Tom to Petty Officer again, when this Swede joins as Mate at Rio.'

'Tom's a good hand. He'll accept it.'

'A good seaman.' From Jones, there was no higher compliment. The Master took a long drag at his Havana Havana. 'I'm worried, Jason. I need your … er, advice. Help.'

'*My* advice, Captain?' Throughout the trade, Barnaby was known to be utterly self-sufficient. A failing of his was that he could be told nothing: 'Old Confucius' was what the more unkind of his crew called him.

'This Mr Karatz: a Swede with a Finnish name. I'll *have* to take him. But he's bound to make trouble if he's Stok's man.'

'You've got Hawkins, sir. And the Second and Third, they're harmless, but they'll be loyal, surely?'

'They're inexperienced, easily swayed… But I can run my own ship. It's Hannah I'm worried about.' The sea captain tossed back his port. 'That's why I'm asking for your help.' The piercing blue eyes stared straight through Jason. 'That swine, Stok, will stop at nothing.'

The silence between them lasted a long time before Jason said, '*Wandering Star*'s his ship.'

Barnaby nodded. 'Hannah is one of her officers, and Stok can get at me that way.'

'What can you do about it, Captain?'

'Warn her of the danger she's in. I told you Stok is utterly ruthless. He's convinced that his empire depends on winning the SACOR: he'll do anything to win it.'

'But how can you alert Hannah?' Jason was sitting upright, hands on the worn arms of his chair. 'You can't contact her directly now that that loud-mouthed Buckle has been flown up to the canal to take over command.'

Barnaby rose from his chair and began pacing the empty room, rings of cigar smoke following in his wake. 'I sent her a telex via the British Consul at Balboa. She ought to have it by now, and I should be getting an acknowledgement.' He stopped in front of Jason. 'I've told her to get out as fast as she can. Anywhere. And then to fly home.'

'What can I do, sir?'

'See your Senior RO. Spin him a yarn and get yourself appointed to *Wandering Star*. I want you to protect her.'

Jason stood up and together they walked to the big window. The last crimson reflections were dancing on the waters of the Plate. Jason said, 'Of course. I'll do all I can.'

'Thanks.' Then Barnaby asked quietly, 'Are you going to the SACOR party tomorrow night to celebrate our next leg to Rio? You might find out more about Stok's men or of any more skulduggery.'

'Yes, I'll be going.' Jason was astonished when the old Captain placed an arm about his shoulders. Together, they walked towards the door to the summoned taxi.

'Go straight back to your ship, Jason,' Barnaby told his guest. 'Keep all this to yourself, and don't let anyone suspect that we're in contact with each other. Thanks for coming.'

Jason looked up enquiringly. 'Aren't you coming?'

'No. I'm sleeping here.' Captain Jones turned, then called over his shoulder as he pushed round the swing doors, 'I'll get a good night's sleep here, far from Stok's Mafia.'

The driver of the taxi was lighting up a cigar. '*Señor?*'

'*Al puerto,*' Jason said in his best Spanish. '*A navegar el Sherrilee.*' He leaned back in the shadows. From now on, he would be living with fear until the drama was over. He felt safe at sea: it was in the ports that death lurked, he thought.

CHAPTER ELEVEN: TOM HAWKINS, BO'SUN

Windrose's three petty officers kept themselves to themselves, content merely to watch, from their less raucous corner in the dancehall, the antics of their fellow-seafarers. The Mayor's reception, buffet supper, and now the disco for the SACOR crews were turning out better than anyone had hoped.

'It's the shared trauma of The Horn,' Sam Tyler, the Sailmaker, said between gulps of the warm fizzy drink which passed for beer. 'Even the old hands won't forget this last passage.'

'That's only because you've had work to do, Sails,' Bert Hicks, *Windrose's* Carpenter remarked. 'How many sails have you made this time?'

'Aw, belt up, Chippy.' The peacemaker was Tom Hawkins, the Bo'sun. He was glad to be among his friends again in the guise of Bo'sun, even for this one evening. He was unhappy with his temporary role as an officer and would be thankful when the relief Mate joined at Rio. He kept his thoughts to himself while watching the SACOR crews cavorting on the dancefloor with their swaying girls.

'Odd,' Sails mused. 'They touch each other when they dance nowadays. Different in my day.'

'Randy old beggar,' Bert Hicks observed. 'You'd be more like that lot, I'll bet.' He nodded towards an Italian from *Stella Venus* who was stationary in the middle of the floor, a *señorita* moulded to him, her arms circling his neck while they kissed, oblivious to the world. The three friends watched admiringly.

Eventually, Tom Hawkins asked, 'What's the new hand like: the bloke from Global who's replaced poor old Plomer?' He did not miss the glance which passed between his two friends.

'Harbin, the new hand? Too old, we reckon, to be a genuine ordinary seaman. Knows his job too well,' Chippy responded.

'A bastard, *I* reckon,' Sails added. 'Something don't add up with him.' He emptied his glass and held out his hand for the other two empties. As he left them, he reinforced his opinion. 'I reckon he's a sea lawyer. Chips, tell Tom what your lad passed on to you.' Sails vanished in the throng crowding the long bar.

'Stevie's my apprentice, Tom; he says that Harbin's wasted no time stirring up trouble in the mess. Calls us a killer ship.'

'Don't the others shut him up?' Tom asked.

'He's a big bloke. Anyway, no one falls for it.'

'Not yet,' Tom answered thoughtfully. 'But something always sticks.' He grinned as a curvaceous *señorita* waggled her hips at him. Then he asked, 'Have you told the Old Man?'

'Not yet. Don't want to worry him,' Chips brooded, peering into the crowd.

'I'll tell him, then,' Tom said. 'I'm keen to cross that finishing line off North Foreland.' They were watching Sails struggling through the press, when the band broke into a rumba. Tom jumped up and forced his way through the swarm of writhing dancers: Sails was balancing the glasses of beer as if he were lurching on a rolling deck. It was then that Tom noticed that same Race Observer whom he had run across at Wellington. Mercer, wasn't he? An ex-Shell deck officer? Cheered to see another Englishman, Hawkins approached the RO as the band changed the tempo.

'Come and join us,' he shouted above the racket. 'Over here...'

The tall fellow nodded and smiled, jerking his head downwards at the girl swaying in his arms, her head level with his chest.

'I'll be over…'

It was past one o'clock in the morning when finally the *Windrose* petty officers decided that they had had enough. Jason was thankful that at last it was over; on their walk back to their ship, Sam Tyler, the Sailmaker, insisted that Jason should accompany them because *Sherrilee* was in the same corner of the dockyard as *Windrose*, albeit on the opposite wharf. It was not long before they were singing the ditty which haunted them all, the song which had even reached the 'Top Ten'; and, with the publicity which SACOR was collecting, the song was being whistled, sung and hummed everywhere. Jason was becoming fed up with it:

'From New Zealand
To Old England,
From anywhere
To anywhere;
The wind is free
And free for me…'

And then they bellowed the chorus:

'Blow the wind, blow;
Blow the wind, blow;
Blow the wind, blow;
Blow the wind, blow!'

It was an evocative tune and once the race was over, whenever he heard it in the future, it would remind him of these exciting days. His friends were insisting on the other verses:

'Windmill, Flettner;
Wingsail, Rotor;
Windship, Dyna;
Kite or schooner…
The wind is free,
And free for me.'

They roared the refrain until Jason became anxious that the police would be called by the occupants of the dingy houses flanking this narrow street leading down to the port. Damn their eyes, Sails and Tom were at it again:

'Sailormen feel
Kick of the wheel;
Quick on your feet,
Aft the mainsheet;
The wind is free,
And free for me.

Blow the wind, blow;
Blow the wind, blow;
Blow the wind, blow,
Blow the wind, blow!'

Sails, who was merrier than his companions, insisted on linking arms; and so, rolling down the middle of the empty street, they eventually sighted the gates of the yard coming up ahead. Someone swore at them from a cafe, but the rare onlooker seemed inclined to join in the fun. When they were a couple of hundred yards from the gate, Tom Hawkins halted the procession while Chippy lit up a cigar. As the match flared in the semi-darkness, Jason spotted a posse of ruffians gathered in the shadows against the wall of a house at the corner of the unlit cross-road. There must have been a dozen of them, and a menacing bunch they looked.

'Watch out, Tom,' Jason warned softly. 'Stick to the middle of the road. Run…'

'Like riggers,' Sails yelled as he began sprinting for the gate, his head low, his arms going like pistons, Jason and Chippy following.

'Get moving!' Tom yelled. 'Go on, I'll cover you…'

As Jason ran for the sanctuary of the gateway, he glanced over his shoulder. The advancing ruffians could not have been more than twenty yards off. There was a grotesque horror about their stockinged faces as, crouching low and brandishing glinting knives, they rushed the fleeing Englishmen. From the far side of the cross-road a large, grey Chevrolet suddenly lurched … and one of them was waving a gun at Hawkins.

'Tom! For God's sake, *come on*…' Jason yelled frenziedly. 'They'll cut you off…'

The Chev swerved and charged between Hawkins and the gate, separating him from the others and the dockyard guard who was blowing his whistle frantically. The rear wing of the car clouted Jason's left thigh and knocked him off balance. He splayed on the gritty road and by the time Hicks had hauled him to his feet, the desperadoes had bundled the berserk Tom into the car. Its tyres squealed. By the time the guard had pulled himself together and doubled back to the gatehouse, the Chevrolet had vanished down the street.

Shocked and out of breath, Jason, Sails and Sam Tyler stood powerlessly next to the stunned guard who was screaming down the phone. An hour later, Jason finally reached *Sherrilee*. The police had been useless. They seemed resentful at being called out at this hour and, despite the Englishmen's furious protestations, had refused to do anything until normal office hours began at nine o'clock. Graft and protectionism were reputed to be rife in the city so, aghast and helpless, Jason and his two companions rushed back to their ships.

Jason ran round the end of the dock to *Sherrilee* on the other wharf. It would be safer to ring Barnaby from the ship, rather than use a docks' phone. For God's sake, *why* had Tom Hawkins, *Windrose*'s fine Bo'sun, been hijacked? Tom's kidnapping and the fears which Captain Jones harboured for his daughter, Hannah, were incidents which centred around *Windrose* and bore the same stamp: were they coincidental? Was someone trying to stop *Windrose* from sailing? And was Stok's Mafia-like organization behind it all, including Mirson's murder in Wellington?

CHAPTER TWELVE: ROLLING UP TO RIO

Acting on Jason's phone call, Barnaby Jones had returned immediately on that Monday night to *Windrose*, where he summoned the police chief and kicked up as much of a furore as he could at that late hour. Despite also hauling in the Consul, there was no trace of Tom Hawkins. During all that Tuesday, the enquiries had continued, but it was not until twilight on the eve of the Montevideo start that the police found the abandoned Chevrolet on a rubbish tip to the north of the city. It had been set alight, but the police, unable to identify the charred body inside, could not prevent *Windrose* from sailing, despite her Master's report of his Bo'sun's kidnapping.

Captain Jones had telephoned Jason in *Rêve de l'Avenir*, his message being terse and guarded: on no account must Jason be connected with *Windrose*; when they reached Rio, he must shift heaven and earth to become appointed RO to *Wandering Star*. Of Hannah Jones there was still no news, but Barnaby might hear something from her on *Windrose*'s arrival at Rio de Janeiro, on Saturday, 20 July. *Wandering Star*'s expected time of arrival at Kingston, Jamaica, was on the same day.

The tragedy of Hawkins' murder hung like a dark cloud over the starters lining up in the River Plate, on that Wednesday, 17 July. All their ensigns were at half-mast and, though Jason Mercer was shocked and appalled by Tom's death, he was glad to have been appointed to this lively French ship, *Rêve de l'Avenir*. He liked Commandant Loic Pennac, a leathery-faced

Breton who knew his job. His demeanour exuded confidence as he paced athwartships the bridge of his prodigious command.

Like everything about this catamaran-ship of the new millennium, the bridge epitomized the most developed technology afloat. The control-room in which Jason stood was a streamlined pedestal ten metres above the spatial observation compartment, a projection which, thrusting forward from the main accommodation joining the two catamaran hulls, hung poised, a protruding half-moon, above the seas. Her owners and designers had calculated that her high-speed advantage would more than justify her exorbitant capital cost. Up here on the navigation bridge (in their V-shaped complex, the radar and communication offices were perched even higher) Jason found it difficult to absorb the gigantic dimensions of this incredible vessel. His stomach still sank, as it always did when, in an instant of vertigo, he would glimpse over a high, sheer cliff. Those midget white horses, those waves flecking beneath the bridge between the two 'cats', were forty-seven metres beneath him.

Rêve de l'Avenir's owners had faced up to the challenge of the oil crisis. It was decided that if their company was to survive, enough capital must be pumped into it to put their sail-assisted ship ahead of her power-driven competitors. Above all, she had to cost less than what she could earn; she must be an above-water ship capable of sustaining her efficiency in relative winds from 5 to 40 knots; the shape of her hull must minimize leeway yet keep the ship as upright as possible; and she must be capable of standing up to all weathers.

Rêve de l'Avenir was the result. A giant catamaran, with her two hulls each 300 metres long, she was built to vanquish her rivals of 120,000 tons. *Rêve de l'Avenir* with her full cargo of twelve hundred 40-foot containers, had a loaded displacement of 124,064 tons. Her 'cats' drew only 14 metres; she had a beam of 60 metres and this virtually barred her from going alongside in most major ports. Jason could see, abaft her starboard aerofoil, one of her cranes which was part of her loading and discharging arrangements.

'*Quel moment merveilleux!*' Pennac glanced at his Race Observer and smiled as he added in his best English, 'You English are still our sole *concurrents* at sea, Monsieur.'

'*Concurrents*, Commandant?'

'The Captain means *competitors*, sir,' the Mate chipped in from the starboard doorway leading to the bridge wing, a wing which seemed hung in space above the muddy El Plato. His English was perfect, his accent barely detectable. Emile Crosier was small and compact, a self-contained man with a mischievous twinkle in his eyes which held the blueness of the Atlantic. Gerard Leduc, the Second, in tie and shirt-sleeves was busy working over his chart at the back of the bridge. The Third, Gaston Fouquier, was down on the starboard hull checking that the anchor and cables were secured for sea.

'They have to do it now,' Captain Pennac observed in a showy French accent. 'Too dangerous at sea.' Jason walked out to the starboard wing where the morning sun was burning up the last of the mists curling in from the estuary. The start was in less than half an hour and *Rêve de l'Avenir* was deliberately being kept until last, because of her beam and unhandiness at slow speeds. There were twelve starters, for the vertical turbine ship, *Sao Isabel*, had just made it, after temporary repairs in Punta Arenas. She was an extraordinary sight with those gigantic contraptions fore and aft, revolving steadily in the breeze. Her vertical sails were two hoops which, by revolving, drove the turbine to make electricity. *Sao Isabel*'s system differed from the American, *Californian Rose*, who had opted for the Panama circuit: her vertical turbine system drove the propeller shaft through reduction gearing. *Sao Isabel* also breathed the gaiety of the Portuguese, her hull bright yellow, her 'sails' red and green. She would be the first in this controlled start to cross the line: it was 1028 and she was running up to it now, on this Wednesday, 17 July. Her crew waved as she passed and from 'tween decks floated the strains of a *carioca*.

'*Il est beau*,' Loic Pennac said, coming out to the wing. He focused his binoculars on the apparition. 'It is a monster.' He shook his head with incredulity.

And so, as the gigantic French catamaran ship drifted to leeward, ships of the SACOR fleet took their turn for the controlled start, a quarter of an hour between ships. After the Portuguese came *Sherrilee*, her for'd 'sail' now repaired and swinging to the wind. Franklin Dicker was waving from the bridge and Jason returned the gesture. In two hours' time, at 1330, it would be *Rêve de l'Avenir*'s turn, but meanwhile he'd stay up here and watch the others go: *Pollux*, the German with the four dynasails, was the next ship heading for the line.

An orange pillar buoy marked the southern end of the start, a line running due south from Brava Point. He could see the beach and the foreshore, black with crowds to wish the ships *bon voyage*. Behind the golf-course he could see the Carrasco Hotel where Jones had succeeded in upsetting Jason's peace of mind for the remainder of the race. And there was *Windrose*, a beautiful sight...

'She'll be standing well out, don't you think, Mr Mercer?' Emile Crozier was asking the question as they watched *Windrose*, with all plain sail set, running before the wind to the line. She was the first of the square-riggers to start and which route Captain Jones would take was of interest to everyone. With no Bo'sun and regular Mate, Jones would probably choose the easier passage, Jason felt sure: they would all know in five hours' time when they reached the open sea. *Windrose* was the trend-setter, but Barnaby was keeping his cards close to his chest.

'The less tacking the better for *Windrose*,' Jason replied. 'She'll stand well out with a quartering wind until she can fetch Rio against the north-easterlies. She'll have to contend with the Brazil current dead against her, if she keeps tacking up the inshore route.'

'She's a fine sight,' said Crozier.

And as *Windrose* crossed, every stitch of canvas set, the cruise clipper, *Reina de la Mar*, hardened up to follow in the British barque's wake. The Spanish passenger ship had stood up to the weather, only half a dozen couples, it was rumoured, having forfeited their berths after the perils of the Cape Horn storm.

'They take a lot of beating,' Jason said, nodding towards the Pole, *Wicher*, who was going about, a mile to windward. She would be the last of the square-riggers before the fore-and-aft schooner, *Sea Falcon*, the Yank schooner who had come through relatively unscathed round The Horn. Jason could not but reflect, as he watched the slick tacking of the schooner, how her near-sister, *Wandering Star*, was progressing those thousand miles to the north.

After the square-riggers crossed the line, the 190,000-ton Singaporean, *Ocean Kite*, would follow with her new battery of kites tugging her out of the Plate estuary; and *Dynasaur*, the monster, two-masted Belgian dynaship who had somehow managed her repairs on time. She was to be the penultimate starter and Jason could see her drifting out of Port Lobos, a breath-taking sight with her symmetrical 'sails', like pyramids and towering to the clouds. And last, after her, *l'Avenir*...

'Have you heard how *Mina* is doing?' the Mate asked. 'The Dutch Flettner?'

Jason nodded. 'She's repaired her rotor.'

'They reckon her stabilizers failed,' Crozier said, shaking his head. 'But I suppose this is the only way to make design progress at sea.' He shrugged his shoulders in that typical Gallic gesture of his. He spread wide his arms and regarded their revolutionary *Rêve de l'Avenir*. 'Someone has to show the way. *Mina* nearly paid the price. Once before, she rolled so badly that both her towers touched the sea in a trough. *Californian Rose*, in that storm off Chile, was trying to take advantage of the Humboldt current for Panama.' Once again, that shrug of the shoulders. 'She got a fright when the tips of her blades touched,' Crozier added.

'Poor devils,' Jason muttered. 'Must have been a rotten moment: lucky for *Mina* that the Dutch build strong ships.'

'*Californian Rose* and *Siddartho* have now retired from the race. *Techno Victory* was lucky to get away with it, wasn't she?'

'Miraculous,' Jason agreed. 'Her Master was flown up from Port Stanley to take over *Wandering Star*.'

'Buckle,' Crozier said. 'He must have quite a reputation with his Owner.'

Emile added, 'The Panama contingent all sailed at dawn from Kingston today. I read my Satnews, Mr Mercer.'

Many of today's starters had anchored overnight in the Montevideo — Port Lobos anchorage. This had given them a chance to overhaul their cranes and derricks because, on arrival at Rio, each ship had to discharge four containers and load six: another SACOR test.

And so the forenoon slipped slowly past, *Rêve de l'Avenir* impatiently waiting for her ultimate place. Jason inspected her from stem to stern, taking his readings and entering his log. The work took his mind off his unsatisfactory interview with the Senior Race Observer, Blair Hamilton, who had been so helpful at Wellington. Blair was tired after his Falklands flight and irritated by the minutiae piling up around him.

'Why, Mercer, should I tamper with my ROs' appointments?' he demanded over the rim of his whisky glass. 'Give me one good reason.'

'I *must* do a trip with *Wandering Star*. I'm scheduled for her, so why not now, sir?'

'*Must* doesn't come in my book, Mercer. You can carry on to your French ship.'

And so the Hamilton meeting terminated: Hamilton bad tempered and Jason frustrated beyond words.

The Mate of *l'Avenir* was speaking into the mic, calling the hands. Five minutes later the great commercial catamaran was setting her extensible 'sails'. He walked out onto the port wing to watch Commandant Pennac and his officers close-hauling the ship. He tucked himself away into a corner, but apart from the men doubling up the container's securing chains on the well of the upper deck, no one was to be seen.

The ship was the largest catamaran yet built for commercial use, the prototype of her class. As the sails hardened to the breeze, Jason felt the great vessel beginning to make way through the water. Commandant Pennac disliked using his engines, and, by reputation, was an excellent ship-haulier.

Rêve de l'Avenir was driven by two batteries of telescopic sails, five athwartships, for'd, just abaft the futuristic bridge; and five aft, their mast steps sunk into the athwartship structure holding the two cat hulls together. To the uncanny silence of hydraulic power, the twenty-seven-metre high sails of flexible plastic sheeting slid upwards from their aerofoil-shaped envelopes which were trimmed to the same angle as the upper sails. The whole battery (there were five sails abreast) was trained in azimuth by powerful motors in watertight compartments below the upper deck, in the same way as the wingsail in *Sherrilee* had been. This new species of vessel was dubbed a *windcat*.

Rêve de l'Avenir was the most remarkable ship in which Jason was ever likely to sail. She was highly sensitive and could answer to the smallest adjustment, she was so finely balanced. She flew like the wind, as Crozier had put it, and could reach twenty-five knots with ease. She sailed much closer to the wind than a square-rigger, even closer than the schooners, but Pennac was keeping secret how close she could come: 45° … 50° off the wind? On the wind, she was a flyer; with her configuration, cargo-stowage and stability, she seemed to be years ahead of her rivals.

Her 1200 containers were all temperature-controlled through a computer. Her auxiliary engines were sited in the after section beneath the after sails, a diesel being in each hull. Like all the assisted ships, she would be close-hauled most of the time. The unknown factor was the length of her life which, because of the enormous stresses, might be less than a traditional hull: this, plus the astronomical cost of building, must weigh against her at the finish, thought the RO as he watched Cape Brava coming abeam.

Jason shared the pride of the Bretons as they cheered their ship when crossing the start line. The wind made a strange fluting sound as the sails were eased before the following wind. *Windrose* was already hull-down, only her royals showing as patches of white above the horizon. She was going well, and it would be five hours before *Rêve de l'Avenir* could begin beating to windward close to the coast. That was the point of sailing she preferred and she would soon be leaving the others standing.

Three days of this exhilarating sailing, Jason realized, but three days nearer Rio, Belém and helping Hannah Jones. And then the trauma of another ship… The Swede, Karl Karatz, *Windrose*'s prospective Mate, would be waiting to join and Jason wondered what sort of a fellow Barnaby would be dealing with.

Jason was soon to find out. Three days later, on the jetty where he landed in Rio, a brutish giant with a black, unkempt beard was kicking his heels. Grabbing his baggage, he elbowed his way down to the launch, before Jason and its passengers had even mounted the steps. The Swede jumped into the service boat and barked at the coxswain to take him to *Windrose*. Looking down from the wharf, Jason made up his mind. Barnaby Jones would need backing, and Jason would do all he could.

CHAPTER THIRTEEN: NEPTUNE'S MASK

Hannah Jones and Jasmine Htut had joined the other three women who were in the shade of the chart house. For this Crossing-the-Line ceremony, Doreen Murray, the Ship's Chief Steward, was insisting that all the *Star*'s females should agree on how best to handle the horseplay which this age-old ritual always generated. 'This isn't my first effort,' she told them, as she fixed her eye on the two girls, Rita and Peggy, who, aged nineteen and twenty, were working their first passage as stewardesses for Global Sea Transport. 'Give 'em so much as a wink,' she added, 'and they'll assume the best.' She smiled, but only with her mouth; her blue eyes remained diamond-hard, thought Hannah.

It was five thirty on the evening of Saturday, 27 July, and in an hour and a half that pulsating sun would be plunging behind those distant purple uplands of the Serra de Tumucumaque which were the frontier between Brazil and Guyana, Surinam and French Guyana. Doreen had brought up a jug of iced grapefruit juice and they were relaxing while waiting for the fun to begin. 'They'll ply us with enough booze when the party starts,' she told them. 'Our Randy knows all the tricks, so watch out, girls.'

Wandering Star had been beating against a north-easterly for these last two hundred miles to the Amazon delta. She was now close-hauled on the port tack, having been headed by the South-East Trades, and Buckle was holding her to fifty-mile tacks: she was loving it, this graceful ship. It was exhilarating stuff for Hannah: all canvas set and the sheets afted on the winches as hard as João Otaz dared, now happy again as Mate. The rigging thrummed and as the hull sliced through the sparkling seas, curtains of spume drifted down her length, to dust her staysails and five mainsails. *From outboard she must be presenting a glorious sight*, Hannah thought to herself. Her tall masts and slender lines, her dark green hull glistening as she lurched from the troughs to shake herself, the spray leaping high, then drifting in clouds to leeward...

Hannah excused herself and slithered to the starboard quarter where the sea, barely three feet below the bulwarks, was hissing like a pressure cooker.

Over to the west, the shore was a grey-green strip. An angry line-squall was drifting northward, but for over twenty-four hours *Wandering Star* had avoided the torrential downpours which had caught her when making the passage between Trinidad and Tobago. Visibility had shut down to nil, and it had been a tricky few hours dodging the shipping in that busy channel. That route had been better than risking the Serpent's Mouth, a challenge which Buckle only just resisted, thank the Lord... But now it was the weather which was getting them all down: the increasingly high humidity as they approached the Equator was bringing out the prickly heat and 'dhobi's itch', as sailors delicately described the skin irritations. It was 28° Celsius, even with this steady wind cooling them down. What would it be like on the Equator at Belém? Only 320 miles to go, that was all...

It seemed another life now, since the *Star* had arrived off Jamaica; but that beautiful island was being ruined by politics and poverty. How seductive the approaches had looked, with the palms swaying along the foreshore, the lavender-blue mountains an ethereal backdrop behind. At dawn, *Wandering*

Star was at the entrance to Port Royal and, with the pilot on board, was proceeding under engine past Plum Point light. Burn Tinewood, friendly now, though enigmatic, and Hannah were piloting the ship up the difficult channel into Kingston Harbour, the anchorage being protected by a narrow strip of grey scrub-covered land.

Remnants of the old naval dockyard were still identifiable at the western end of this peninsula on which the old Port Royal was built. The entrance led past islets of scrub-topped mud-flats steaming in the torrid heat, to the leading mark of the old Fort Augusta. Tinewood and Hannah were relieved when finally they laid down their dividers on the chart, the *Star* having negotiated the last of the shallows to secure alongside the rotten timber wharf at the end of the old railway jetty.

The capital of Kingston lay at the feet of the Blue Mountains. Built on the low-lying plain which must once have been lush with tropical vegetation, the city, despite its American hotel towers, now sprawled like a squid, a motley of brightly coloured houses vying with the shacks of shanty-town. The amorphous jumble was shrouded by a slowly rising mist, and the beauty of the island gave Hannah a longing to get ashore as soon as she could.

Burn Tinewood had unloaded all the mail on to her, a chore which kept her busy until mid-afternoon. The heat then overwhelmed her, and she slept until six o'clock in the small steel box which was her cabin. By then the ship had watered, so she freshened up under the shower for her run ashore with Jasmine Htut, who was waiting impatiently for her on the upper deck. They were having dinner together at the Myrtle Bank, the old colonial hotel which lived on its reputation of the bygone age when the island was garrisoned by British forces. But as she was joining Jasmine at the gangway, Burn

Tinewood bore down upon her from the poop deck: there was malice in his eyes as he handed over to her a three-week backlog of chart corrections; the 'orders' file from Global Sea Transport.

'The Captain insists on your finishing these tonight, Miss Jones,' he said. 'However late you work,' he added with a malevolent leer. He turned to Jasmine who, embarrassed, did not know where to look. 'I'll give you dinner, Jasmine,' he said, his face creasing into a smile. 'The Myrtle Bank has a pool. Bring your swim suit: it's hot and there's a moon.'

Hannah met Jasmine's apologetic and resigned glance as she preceded Burn down the gangway. Fuming with resentment, Hannah changed back into her catsuit and worked until she finished the corrections at three on Sunday morning.

It was 21 July and not only was she 'duty' officer, but she was too whacked even to go ashore. And all that day, whenever she ran across the loathsome Buckle, she was repelled by the secretive, sly smile lurking in his eyes and crimping the corners of his mouth, a prissy mouth lost in the bushy, ginger beard. She despised the way he looked at her, feeling naked when she sensed him behind her as she worked alone at the chart table.

Hannah wrenched her mind from the past. She must concentrate on the present and what lay ahead when they reached Belém. Whatever happened, she had to contact her father; she had succeeded in slipping a ten-dollar bill into the pilot's hand as he was leaving at Plum Point. She had murmured her request for him to send the telex which she had prepared, and he had nodded discreetly.

Anthony Hope and his Ruritanian classics, *The Prisoner of Zenda* and *Rupert of Hentzau*, had once been among her dad's favourites. Her telex read:

Please advise Tony hope will meet me arrival UK.
Signed Hannah Adnez.

Her dad enjoyed his crosswords so would have little difficulty in deciphering the message. In twenty-four hours' time, *Wandering Star* would be arriving at Belém, and her dad would be there. The police, perhaps...? And she remembered the Race Observer too, that tall, fair-haired merchant navy officer who had been in Shell with her dad, Jason Mercer... With a half-smile playing on her lips, she contemplated the antics which were starting amidships for the Crossing of the Line...

In every ship, there is always a comedian. In the *Star*, the fo'c'sle claimant to this role was Fred, the able sailor who virtually ran the crew, whatever the Bo'sun's views were. And as Hannah watched, Neptune himself was being hauled over the starboard gunwale. To the cheers of all, the King of the Oceans, complete with trident and webbed feet, was being installed on his throne between Tuesday and Wednesday masts: *Wandering Star's* five masts being named, from for'd, after the weekdays.

Despite the spun-yarn beard glued to the beaming face, it was not difficult to identify Neptune as the Ship's Bo'sun: the king of the denizens of the deep sported a golden cardboard crown; his scuba-suit and flippers were traced with silver-painted scales. Neptune was about to administer justice to one of his recalcitrant citizens grovelling before him, a tousled lady in a seaweed mini-skirt who, Jasmine whispered to Hannah, curiously resembled Fred. And, in a trice, Fred was to be punished traditionally by having his straggly locks hacked off by Neptune's retainers. This was Fred's first Crossing of the Line and first entering of Neptune's kingdom... It was good, thought Hannah, to be able to join in the laughter, for fun seemed to be at a premium at the moment.

'Come on, Hannah,' Jasmine was murmuring into Hannah's ear. 'We'd better join in this fun and games or the Fo'c'sle will take it out of us.' Her eyes were searching Hannah's for support. 'Sailors aren't all bad, you know.'

'That's not what you told me after Kingston,' Hannah retorted. 'Forgotten the Myrtle Bank already?'

Jasmine shook her head. 'Burn drank too much. Anyone can do that.'

'Okay. Then you can lead the way up for'd.' Hannah watched the nurse sidling to the fo'c'sle where the crew were assembled for King Neptune's ritual. Hannah was restless: she was convinced now that she was a prisoner in the hands of this mutable and ostentatious Master and some of his officers. It was the sinister atmosphere which scared her: no one would answer her questions straightforwardly, and all her requests to see Buckle officially had gone unheeded. She would confront him verbally as soon as she could: a difficult thing to engineer in these close quarters, especially as she preferred not to be caught alone with this man who had obviously earned his nickname. While she idly watched the sails thrashing when the ship went about to the other tack, she took her mind off her fears by ruminating on the theoretical possibilities which future technology might harness to move cargoes about the world.

The most unlikely lark in the SACOR race, thought Hannah, was *The Ark*. This competitor, allowed to take part for the fun of it, should already be a quarter of the way across the Atlantic. The longer that that floating greenhouse took over the voyage, the better, so that the plants she was propagating and saving for mankind could germinate and become established. Perhaps

The Ark's courageous demonstrations might appeal enough to the world's imagination for its peoples to become enraged that their planet was being biologically raped. Chemical agriculture, world-wide deforestation; the 'hoovering-up' of every living organism which could swim in the oceans; the poisoning of the planet by industrial wastes and oil spillages: all these practices were leading with lemming-like inevitability to the extinction of plant, bird, insect and animal until the world cried, 'Enough!' *The Ark* and her successors could save threatened species.

If it was practical economically for cargoes to remain longer at sea, it was feasible theoretically to use the ocean currents, as *Plant Earth*, the huge raft, was doing. In theory, too, buoyancy could be used to move hulls: if a commercial submarine floated up from the bottom of the ocean, she could exploit that surfacing energy to propel her way in any direction. On reaching the surface, she could use gravity to sink again to the seabed ... and so on, *ad infinitum*.

Ships sailing around the tropical latitudes could use solar energy to provide a quarter of the power required to propel a 135-metre ship, even at today's state of the game. And wave power, which had been used for years to generate energy for specialist needs such as the lighting of navigational buoys, was already being harnessed to drive small craft: one day, it might be possible to propel a 400-ton ship at 15 knots. Other than wind power, two natural resources remained: the lines of magnetic force, and gravity. Newton's law of universal gravity defined it, but the masses needed for mutual attraction at sea were too great: two 10,000-ton ships with their centres of gravity 61 feet apart would attract each other with a force of four and a half pounds. Theory fascinated Hannah, but like some of the ships who had come to grief already on this SACOR, scientific probability was a world apart from the realities of a gale at sea. Hannah's spirits lifted from the slough into which they had descended, as she mused on the day ahead.

Windrose, she had read in Sparks' Daily Report, had sailed from Rio on Monday, 22 July, on the same day as the *Star* had sailed from Kingston. She pictured her dad now, legs splayed where he stood on his poop, his old dog, Skate, beside him. He loved the old bitch, the black and white border-collie-Labrador mongrel: they'd been together since Hannah had been a schoolgirl in pigtails. Skate was for Barnacle Jones a link with the wife he had adored.

Hannah felt a tenderness mounting inside her as she watched the crude display going on for'd. Perhaps those melon-bosomed sailors with their stranded, Terylene, homemade wigs were trying to provoke Jasmine and herself. She bit her lip: how could she escape from this enforced surveillance? *Why* were they holding her? If only they would tell her, she would be able to face the uncertainty. And it would help if only Jasmine could understand Hannah's feelings better.

She supposed that behind it all was the lust for money. The Stok empire *had* to win SACOR in order to keep its diesel ships in business; and the astronomical prizes (fifty million American dollars for the overall winner; one million for the first ship over the line) led to ruthlessness: fifty million dollars divided amongst a crew of thirty would go a long way, even for those in the fo'c'sle. She watched Doreen, the stewardess, detaching herself from the bunch of revellers who were already drinking. She murmured something to Tinewood, who was dolled up as Long John Silver, complete with hook. Burn lingered a moment, emptied his glass, then strolled aft towards the wheelhouse.

'Miss Jones…'

She turned towards the hoarse voice she detested. Randy Buckle, dressed up crudely as Amphitrite, Neptune's wife, was leaning against the taffrail; arms akimbo, he surveyed her coolly from the crown of her head to the soles of her feet. 'You'll let me call you Hannah today, won't you?' He guffawed while he watched the colour mounting in her cheeks. 'King Neptune is boss today: no formalities, my dear. No discipline. Just good friends.'

His ingratiating tone irritated her. 'I'll stay formal, so long as you remain my Captain.'

The lids drooped over his eyes. Only the lower half of his pupils showed, two flickering specks of light. She felt he was taunting her, playing with her, like a cat with a crippled bird. 'Well, *Miss* Jones, if that's the way you want to play it. A pity: I was hoping to avoid unpleasantness. By the way,' he added sharply, 'you *are* "Bligh" Jones's daughter, aren't you?'

She said nothing, trying to conceal the momentary surprise.

'You might as well admit it,' he snapped. 'Anyway, I'm assuming that you are.'

'Captain Buckle,' Hannah replied, drawing herself up to her full five feet four, her words sounding ridiculously pompous, 'You have authority over your officers, but you can't keep me on board against my will. Tomorrow I'll be contacting the Senior Race Observer at Belém. Your present incumbent is hopeless: you've managed to keep him drunk the whole of the trip since Cristóbal.'

'Hendriks likes his Bols,' Buckle grinned. 'Come on, Hannah, don't be so aggressive. Come to my cabin. I've a confidential signal for you.'

'For me?'

'Came by Satcom on the 1500 routine.' He bowed mockingly, swept his hand in gracious salute. 'After you, ma'am.'

She felt his breath on the nape of her neck when she trotted down the ladder. She smelt the whisky and she realized he was already the worse for wear. It was sombre out of the blinding sun; the silence hit her too, the drumming of the wind in the shrouds and the slatting of the canvas suddenly gone. She turned left and paused before the Master's cabin.

'After you...' He leaned across to open the door. She recoiled, saw the resentment in his face. He pushed her abruptly across the step. She would have fallen had not an arm caught her from behind the door: a forearm with a hideous hook strapped to it.

'Ho-ho, me beauty!' It was Burn Tinewood's laugh. 'Gotcha...'

As she jerked away, she heard the door slam behind her, its lock slatting home. She spun round. Unable to identify the sickly odour pervading the spacious cabin, she saw Doreen standing in front of her, a smirk at the corner of her lips. The stewardess bent over a table upon which was a tray, a phial, cotton wool and a syringe. *Ether...*

There was a *clang!* as Tinewood heaved his steel hook into the corner of the cabin. Grabbing Hannah, he pinioned her arms behind her. She started to scream. Buckle turned up the radio; Burn clapped a hand across her mouth. She sank her teeth into the flesh, tasted the salty, warm blood. Then, threshing frenziedly to avoid the needle, she sent the table crashing to the deck. She felt Buckle's hands on her, screamed when the hypodermic jabbed through her trousers and into her thigh. She glimpsed the evil glint in the stewardess's eye ... then knew no more.

CHAPTER FOURTEEN: AMAZONIAN SENTINEL

On Thursday evening, 25 July, at 1756, the lighthouse of Cape Calcanhar was drawing abeam to port of the French catamaran-ship, *Rêve de l'Avenir*. Commandant Loic Pennac was crouched over the port wing repeater, his eye glued to the prism while waiting for the Cape to draw abeam. At his elbow, his 'First', Emile Crozier, was idly watching the aerofoil mainsails as the big futuristic cat-ship punched into the flying spume. The ship lay to her lee hull, the seas hissing along her gunwales while hard on the wind and close-hauled, she beat to windward. And as Jason Mercer regarded both men, his spirits soared with the exhilarating motion of this huge, twin-hulled ship so many years ahead of her time. With her 'sails' sheeted in as hard as the Mate dared, the ten aerofoils were driving her at twenty-four knots: this was something he had never dreamed possible and probably would never experience again … not bad for a 124,000-ton ship, fully loaded with uranium ore and her 1,400 'boxes' of general cargo.

'*Babord dix … faites le cap, trois-zéro-zéro,*' called out Pennac. He straightened up and nodded at Emile Crozier, who repeated the order into the mic. The winch operator eased over the servo control; the 'sails' checked swiftly; smoothly and silently the extensile aerofoils canted towards the port beam while the ship swung to her new course. It was impressive stuff, and Jason never grew weary of watching the precision with which this vessel was handled. Every man, from the Captain downwards, was proud of his ship who, all the way up the

Brazilian coast, was trouncing her rivals. No other ship could sail as close to the wind; her fine lines and 'cat' hulls were making mincemeat of the adverse currents. She was now seven miles off the Cape, with the islets of Rocas and Fernando de Noronha one hundred miles to the nor'-east.

Commandant Pennac's leathery face was creased in a grin when he invited all, save the officer of the watch, for '*un verre*' in his sea cabin. He waited until the ship had settled to the following wind, but now her motion was entirely different. Running before the dying breeze, *Rêve de l'Avenir* was wallowing in the long swell; her rigid 'sails' were bouncing, as she yawed fifteen degrees on either side of her course. Pennac swore beneath his breath as he led the way to his cabin. Emile pushed Jason in ahead, as the white-coated steward eased the cork from the Mumm's champagne bottle.

They were into the second glass when the 'call' buzzer bleeped above the Captain's desk. Pennac leaned towards the speaker, then angrily snapped it off. Grabbing his cap, he hurried from the cabin, his officers scurrying after him to the starboard wing of the semi-circular bridge. The ship was yawing badly and, at every trough, was spilling the wind: she was making only three knots, though the wind was still Force 4. Pennac cursed rarely, but a string of Gallic oaths burst from his lips. With a morose grin which he hurriedly concealed, Emile Crozier handed his binoculars to the RO.

It took Jason only seconds to focus on the three white 'royals' tipping the horizon to the north-east. And as he watched, the head of the fore topgallant began to climb above the line of grey-blue ocean which delineated the horizon.

'*Windrose*,' he muttered.

'Can't mistake her,' Crozier murmured, out of his Captain's hearing. 'A beautiful vessel.'

They did not return to the Captain's cabin. Instead, while the sun plunged into the west and the light faded, dinner was retarded so that they could watch the British five-masted barque overhaul them from the eastward. By the end of twilight, *Windrose* was almost abeam, her port light burning brightly as she swept past them, less than a mile and a half to starboard. Pennac stomped from the bridge to dine by himself. He still refused to make use of his engines, after having done so well for the past three days.

Rêve de l'Avenir did not reach the Bay of Guajará, Belém, until Wednesday, 31 July. At five minutes after noon Jason was wedged into the only shady corner on the starboard side of the bridge roof. From there he could see the big ships, *Hijaz* and *Ocean Kite*, and watch the growing armada coming into view, while the giant French catamaran slid towards the outer line of vessels swinging in the swirling estuary of the Amazon.

An hour later, *Rêve de l'Avenir*'s anchor plunged into the yellow-brown waters to find the thick mud. She was the last of the fleet to arrive, Commandant Loic Pennac's obstinacy having over-ridden his common sense. He had refused to use his engines: instead, he had taken his ship off to the northward and tacked on broad reaches down the mean line of advance, a tactic which proved successful: she had sizzled along at twenty-five knots on this, her best point of sailing. It had been a memorable two days, but, with the following winds, the catamaran may have lost as many points as she had gained whilst beating up the east coast from Rio.

Jason recoiled from the scorching rail of the bridge wing, and counted the ships in the bay. He then identified those which were tucked into every corner of the docks and berthed along the quays lining the Bay of Guajará which, at its northern end, merged with the Guamá River. The Capim River encircled Belém on its southern side and, as did all the other rivers, drained into the waterway on the southern side of the Island of Marajó. This huge archipelago, with its two thousand islands, was a vast, marshy waste as large as Wales; it formed a plug at the mouth of the Amazon, this most gigantic and impressive of all our planet's rivers. And Belém, the largest port in the north of South America, was the host city: over half a million exuberant Brazilians were now feting the SACOR ships.

Jason could pick out the docks now, gleaming after their modernization to take container traffic. The harbour had been dredged to take the world's biggest ships and four huge container cranes now dwarfed the Castilhos and Marshal Hermes avenues. Before the container era, there had been enough water to take only ships up to 22 feet draught; only those with a maximum displacement of 7,700 tons and a length of 142 metres had been allowed alongside. In those earlier days, the sole crane could lift only 18 tons and 20-feet container dry vans. Rubber from the Amazonian forests had brought wealth, and Belém was now a modern city, with its own major airport linking it to the wide world, with its container terminal, repair yards and dry dock.

Jason was looking forward to getting ashore, to meeting Barnaby Jones for news of his daughter and of Tom Hawkins' murderers. It would be refreshing to savour the Brazilian city which breathed its own culture and pulsated with Amazonian life: Rio de Janeiro had been too much of a tourists' paradise. There was a Hilton too, here at Belém, but the city was too close to the Amazon and the people of its jungles for it to have been destroyed yet by Western civilization. *Rêve de l'Avenir* was swinging to the current and coming to her anchor, half a mile off the Ver-o-Peso, the 'watch-the-weight' market already extolled by the pilot whom they had picked up when entering the bay.

Ashore, the scene was of masts and rigging along the quays fringing the jumbled buildings. Prominent among the forest of spars were those of *Windrose* towering above her neighbour's, the 'turbo-sail' *Jacques-Yves Cousteau*, which the great champion of the sea had developed so successfully. The system was evolved from the German Magnus and Flettner inventions of the twenties: instead of revolving, vertical cylinders to generate the energy, the *Cousteau* was driven by four fixed vertical cylinders, at the tops of which air was injected by small turbos. The resultant lateral component produced forward thrust. Cousteau's first ship, the 'aeolian' *Alcyone*, when sailing with a fifteen-knot beam wind, made nine knots without any fuss. Those successful early days in the eighties had produced this 8,000-ton ship who had transited the Panama Canal. So far she had not experienced any storm weather, and she looked a futuristic designer's dream as her aluminium alloy hull gleamed in the blazing sun.

'*Il est beau aussi, le Cousteau*,' Pennac called across to Jason. The Breton grinned with pride and shook hands when Jason left the bridge with the Belém pilot. The Race Observer had packed his grip hours ago, determined not to miss his first chance of getting ashore. Pennac's obstinacy had lost days of time, and there were now only two days before the next start to Boston. Jason had to pack in a lot before the next 'off', but first he'd report to the Senior RO, Blair Hamilton, for his next ship. The SRO might now be more sympathetic towards Jason's request to join the *Star*, so that he could extricate Hannah Jones from her rotten predicament. She seemed to have her head well fixed on, according to her father.

'*Au revoir, mon Capitaine!*' Jason yelled, as he took off his cap and waved it to the mahogany face leaning through the huge window of the space-ship's bridge. The passage had been interesting and, although the ship had lost precious time during her run up the north coast, she should romp home easily among the leaders to Boston. The French were well in the van of sail-assisted commercial ships: they had a flair for invention and style and, despite whichever political party was in power, France often backed a winner when the nation produced one — unlike the divided British.

Jason's eye was caught once again by *Windrose*, as the pilot cutter bounced across the short sea, kicking up the brown water. The British barque had been one of the first results of Britain's effort to become once again a thrusting, confident industrial nation. *Windrose* was the late-in-time child of young, energetic firms who learned the skills and techniques abandoned when high-tech had taken over. Sailmakers, canvas cloth fabricators, coppersmiths and extinct trades had been re-born to build good British ships again, a direct result of response to that 'Industry Year'. *Windrose*, loaded with wool and containers, looked an aristocrat with her fine lines and taut appearance where she dwarfed her neighbours along the quays. The American seven-masted schooner loaded with silicon, *Sea Falcon*, was overshadowed by *Windrose*'s tall masts.

On the far side of the barque was the vertical turbine *Sao Isabel*, her 18,040 tons taking up much of the precious wharfage. According to the pilot, she was in big trouble with her training motors and might well have to withdraw from SACOR. But *where* was the ship for which he was searching? Surely *Wandering Star* must be in harbour, with all the pull which Stok was capable of exercising.

The little Polish barque, *Wicher,* with phosphates; Spain's *Reina de la Mar,* the British, Colin Mudie-designed and Spanish-built cruise passenger ship; *Storm Petrel,* the Australian six-masted schooner with Kiwi fruit; the German *Pollux* dynaship, carrying coal; *Sherrilee,* with bulk chemical ores; and the Italian kite and ducted-fan ship, *Stella Venus,* full of cars, were all crammed alongside, but no sign of *Wandering Star* ... and as the pilot boat entered calmer water, Jason glanced at the outlines of the ships anchored off: all the big and awkward ones...

Red Star, the Russian-manned Costa Rican, combining a fore-and-aft rig with rigid sails and two dynamasts, was loaded to her marks with mineral ores, and was anchored well out, clear of contamination; ahead of her, the huge Saudi bulker, *Hijaz,* carrying tinned New Zealand lamb, with her nine rigid collapsible Bermudan sails; the giant Singaporean, *Ocean Kite,* 190,000 tons, a grain bulker, with her giant winches; the refrigerated meat carrier, *Dynasaur;* the advanced Flettner *éolienne Jacques-Yves Cousteau,* with coconut oil; Stok's refrigerated fruit carrier, *Techno Phanta,* with her gigantic windmill driving the horizontal turbine; and, finally, to the north and anchored in defiant isolation, the black-hulled *Wandering Star.* The pilot boat swung round and, stemming the current, bumped alongside the steps of the Praça do Relógio.

'*Adios, señor,*' the pilot said. He jerked his head towards the dark clouds billowing in from the north-west. 'Afternoon rain.' He glanced at his watch. 'Come all days.' Grinning, he legged it for the harbour master's offices. 'You get wet, *señor...*'

Fort Castelo frowned down upon the bustling crowd; the time-worn stone of Our Lady of Belém's Cathedral towers smiled upon the port; and with the Governor's Palace and the Prefectura surveilling them, Jason felt that here he was in the bloodstream of the real Brazil. He turned left and hurried into a bar at the entrance to the Castilhos Avenue. The heat inside, despite the slowly revolving fan, was stifling. Though his tropical shirt and cotton trousers were *de rigueur*, the humidity was not made more tolerable by the choking cigar smoke clouding the dark interior.

He ordered a beer and was searching for a corner seat when an American voice bawled through the gloom: 'Hi Jason!' A slap across the shoulder and there was Franklin Dicker and Jeff Hines, the Mate and Second of *Sherrilee*. While the heavens opened like a water spout, the shipmates put the interlude to good use.

Jason accepted Franklin's invitation to sleep and dine in *Sherrilee*. 'But I've got to report to the Senior RO. See you for dinner, Franklin.'

The pavements were steaming beneath his feet, when the sun burst from behind the clouds. At least the heat was bearable out here in the open, so, with lifting spirits, Jason strode through the bustling market of the Ver-o-Peso, towards the SRO's temporary office on the corner of November Fifteenth Street and Fishermen's Square.

The quays of Ver-o-Peso market were packed with fishing craft, yachts and canoes, the colourful green and red Brazilian flags flying from their masts; white drenched hulls gleamed after the downpour, and lookout ratlines for the tuna fishermen dripped with rainwater. The red clocktower overlooking the port was sounding three o'clock so, although the Boston start was only two days away, there would be plenty of time to call on Captain Jones before this *Sherrilee* evening. He'd dump his bag with Blair Hamilton, for it was too damn hot to cart it wherever he went, and he gripped it more tightly as he shoved his way through the packed market.

It was no wonder that the tourists were drawn to this spectacle: every sort of merchant was here with his stall, with his mat and square yard of pavement, his wares displayed before him. People from the jungle, fishermen from the Amazon, touts inveigling trippers to ride buffaloes or to explore the Amazon and its tributaries in powered canoes. With this, the heaviest rainfall on earth, the fauna was luxuriant; a breeze blew all year round but, despite the heat, the air was pure, even along the waterfront, though Belém was only a hundred miles from the Equator.

The wares of the market stalls were varied: Afro-Brazilian charms, aphrodisiac herbs and love potions brewed from parts of animals and insects; scrapers to gouge out the guarana fruit made from the tongues of the giant pirarucu fish which could weigh a hundred kilos and be two metres long; stalls of ceramics from Marajó Island. The market stank of fish and humanity, but it pulsated with life, in comparison to the concrete sky-scrapers rearing into the blue sky. And from what the pilot had told him, it was their exuberant Christianity which gave these Northern Brazilians their spontaneous friendliness. The annual ceremony of 'The Nazareth Candles' turned out 700,000 worshippers to process on its two-mile walk with the statue of The Virgin from the Basilica of Nazareth. Reaching the green trees behind the market, Jason was relieved to stroll beneath their shade to Blair Hamilton's office.

'That's the best I can do, Mercer: *Windrose*.'

Jason was dismissed. 'Thanks, sir. At least it'll be good to be in a British ship again.'

'Okay. Sorry to bounce you this evening: the Costa Rican RO forgot to register the fuel in *Wandering Star*; I'm missing *Hijaz*'s readings too and I can't accept figures from ship's officers. Can you get me both fuel "dips" by six o'clock, so that I can get the ships' computerized race placings by tomorrow?'

Jason nodded. 'We've only got thirty-six hours. I'll get 'em, sir, but I wish *Avenir* had not been last in. I could have done with a good run in Belém!'

'You can drop *Wandering Star*'s readings in here on your way back from the Bay. Give my respects to Captain Jones.'

'I was going to see him, sir, but I'll be sleeping in *Sherrilee* for the night. I'm joining *Windrose* tomorrow morning.' He stepped out into the dazzling sunlight to retrace his steps to the Harbour Landing, where the service boat would be waiting for him.

The service boat took twenty minutes to reach the Saudi ship: *Hijaz*, with her vast freeboard, was a smart ship, her superstructure white and gleaming. Jason scrambled up her orange side where, at the top, a swarthy seaman escorted him to the chief officer. Ten minutes later, having extracted the fuel readings from the centralized computer, the Mate took him to the British Master. Ten minutes later, at 1645, he was threading his way beneath the rigid Bermudan sails which were dipped from their battery of swan-neck masts. He clattered down the ladder to the boat which shoved off into the short seas and punched towards the furthest ship in the anchorage.

As he watched that black hull growing larger, he began to sense a mixture of emotions. He looked forward to seeing that delightful girl again, but he was uneasy at what he would find. She was obviously very miserable in *Wandering Star*, which, for her, was out of character. Had Jones done anything about her predicament by now? The fact that *Wandering Star*, with Randy Buckle's taste for the bright lights, was anchored so far out in the roadstead, bode ill… But whatever Buckle's reaction, Jason had a valid reason to board her on the SRO's authority. If he, Jason Mercer, could not contact Assistant Navigating Officer Hannah Jones once he was on board, he would eat humble pie. The charts and the ship's track: couldn't he demand to see them too, as well as obtaining the fuel dip?

'You'll lie off, please, and wait for me?' Jason asked. The English-speaking cox'n grinned and lit a cigar; he cupped it in the palm of his hand and, having delivered his passenger, sheered clear to lie off on *Wandering Star*'s starboard quarter.

'Can't you see the yellow flag? No one's allowed on board this ship.'

Ignoring the surly petty officer glowering from the deck, Jason called upwards: 'Of course, I can. I'm the Race Observer and have authority to board.' He started to mount the accommodation ladder. 'D'you want to finish the race? You'd better let me have your fuel readings: otherwise you're disqualified and can't continue with the Boston leg.'

'Bloody hell!' There was no mistaking the raucous voice booming from behind the RO. 'Didn't the Dutch RO take 'em?'

'No.' Jason was going to give as good as he got. 'Are you going to let me have your readings?' He paused on the ladder and half-turned towards his service boat. 'Please yourself. And hurry up.'

Buckle hesitated, then stared contemptuously down at Jason. 'Come on board,' the Master of *Wandering Star* growled. 'And get on with it. I'll fetch the Chief.'

Jason crossed the gangway. Meeting Buckle's eye, he said, 'The Senior Race Observer wants a tracing of your track chart ... can't leave until I've got it.'

Randy Buckle swore foully, then called, 'Follow me: fuel dips first. You can wait here, in the wheelhouse.'

'I'll accompany the Chief Engineer: those are my orders.'

'Stay here, Mercer.'

'Where? Here, on the upper deck?'

'Get in the shade of the wheelhouse. The rest of the ship is out of bounds to you.'

'Why?'

'Because those are my orders,' Buckle shouted, his face flushing. He swore obscenely and flung open the wheelhouse door. 'Wait there in the shade and I'll have the track copied.'

As Jason stepped through the doorway, Buckle, in shorts and red shirt, shuffled aft in his slippers and yelled for his navigating officer. 'Pilot, get off your arse. These bloody ROs want a copy of our track chart from Kingston.'

Out of the sunlight, to Jason's eyes it was almost dark in the wheelhouse. He moved silently, alone for a moment in the empty compartment. When he neared the chart table at the after end of the cramped space, he stopped abruptly. Something was moving on the settee which bordered the after bulkhead. Then someone frail was unsteadily weaving towards him.

'Jason?' the girl's voice whispered. 'Jason…? You're Jason Mercer?' The words were hardly audible. The woman was in front of him and swaying on her feet.

'Hannah — Hannah Jones,' he said softly. 'Yes, it's me, Hannah.'

'Don't touch me.' She recoiled, her eyes staring, her irises black and abnormally large. 'Get away…' She was sobbing and shaking violently.

'Hannah… What are they doing to you?' She seemed so frail, a dim shadow of the Hannah Jones he had last seen. Her sunken eyes were set in yellow pools, her cheeks were drained of colour, drawn and hollow.

'I'll take you with me. *Now...*'

Then he heard Buckle's voice becoming louder from the deck outside.

'No!' she whispered fiercely. 'They'll kill me. Don't, *please*.' She had vanished through the door, so swiftly that he was not sure he was not suffering hallucinations in this appalling heat. The wheelhouse door slid on its tracks and the Ship's Navigator burst inside. His eyes were suspicious as he faced the RO.

'Track chart? Why d'you want it?'

Jason looked blank. 'The Senior Race Observer has sent me out to get one from you. I could have been having a run ashore, instead of spending my only evening in Belém on board your ship.' Jason glared angrily at the aggressive fool. 'What's your name?'

'Tinewood. Second Mate.'

'The SRO will be glad to know it.'

Buckle pushed his way between them. 'Get on with it, Pilot: give the idiot what he wants. We're sailing in two days and...' He poked Jason in the stomach. 'We're going to win this SACOR. Keep out of the way, Mister, and stop poking your nose in... Understand?'

Without a word, Jason stepped back and leaned against the bridge window. 'The track chart? And my fuel readings?'

'Burn: get him the track chart.' Buckle turned angrily and bellowed through the door, 'Chief, for heaven's sake, where are you?'

Jason heard a scuffling down the passageway and then the worried face of the Engineer showed outside the doorway, his 'greaser' beside him, complete with dipping rod.

'Comin' wi' me?' The Chief moved off, cursing silently to himself.

Jason ignored the Master and followed the Engineer down the ladder to the main deck. In five minutes, they had collected the readings; then, without a word, Jason climbed back to the upper deck. He hailed the service boat and, ignoring everyone, scuttled down the gangway. 'Take me ashore, please.'

The cox'n grinned and, cigar still between his lips while the boat rolled downwind towards the harbour, kept silent for as long as he could. Finally, extracting the cigar from his mouth, he spat over the side. 'Liberian ship,' he riled. 'Capitano and sailors…' He gave a demonstrative shrug of his shoulders at the same time as drawing a dirty finger across his throat. 'No gut bastids. No come ashoreside Belém.'

Jason grinned: flags of convenience, apparently, were unpopular in Belém. But his thoughts were on the girl with the frightened eyes. She had refused help, looked drugged.

'Why aren't they coming ashore?' he asked, eager to discover the local's reaction.

The Portuguese language added a musical cadence to the coxswain's torrent of abuse. '*Bastids*' was the most recurrent word in the reply and it was obvious that the natives were holding the ship in contempt. Apparently, *Wandering Star*'s provisioning consisted entirely of booze, the ship being stocked up with canned American food.

The shadows were lengthening when Jason hurried up the stone steps of the harbour master's quay. He kept clear of the crowds: he would collect his grip from the SRO's office, where he would telephone *Sherrilee* to cancel his visit. Barnaby Jones must be told at once what was happening to his daughter.

The walk along the docks was farther than he had reckoned. The smaller ships were berthed in trots on each other; the variety of so many futuristic vessels was unique. From the tiny *Wicher* to the big *Sherrilee* stretched a forest of masts, derricks, samson posts, funnels and furled sails. He slowed his pace as he neared the emerald-green hull of the ship he was beginning to know so well: *Windrose*'s yards smartly trimmed, her sails neatly furled, her gangway manned by a seaman in uniform. He trotted over the brow, returned the salute of a man he could not remember seeing before.

'The Captain, please. Mr Mercer: your next Race Observer.'

The seaman's eyes were suspicious and, for this taut ship, seemed surly. 'Wait there,' he muttered. 'The Mate said no one was to come on board without his say-so.'

'It's the Master I've come to see,' Jason snapped. 'Not the Mate.'

'Stop 'ere, then.'

Jason dumped his bag on the teak deck; seething, he was perplexed by the change in things. The shadows from the braced yards cast across the decks like ebony filigree; the heat from the sun's rays bounced off the surface of the water. The curious silence and empty decks made him uneasy: *Windrose* had always been bustling with cheerful seamen, courteous POs and officers ... but now all he could hear was the mewing of seabirds, while across the quay a dog barked frenziedly as it chased a monstrous, mangey cat.

'Follow me. The Cap'n says he's only got a moment.'

Jason followed the man through the wheelhouse along the route he knew so well. After the dazzling sunlight 'tween decks, the darkness made him falter while he followed his surly guide. The PO stood back, then tapped perfunctorily on the Master's cabin door.

The door was flung open. In the centre of the cabin a giant of a man stood scowling at the intruder. Behind the desk was the familiar figure of Captain Jones. He was slumped in his chair, his shoulders hunched.

'I'll see the Race Observer on his own. Wait outside, Mister.'

Jason had never heard Captain Jones address his officers thus. This new mate was standing his ground. 'Anything you've got to say, Captain,' he said in the guttural accents of the Scandinavian, 'you can say in front of me.'

Jones flushed and sprang to his feet. 'Get out of my cabin,' he rasped. 'Wait outside.' He fixed the Swede with his blazing blue eyes. 'The hands will have to wait.'

The Mate hesitated, then stomped from the cabin. He pulled the door shut behind him.

Barnaby stepped from behind his desk, but his hand was shaking when he extended it to Jason.

'The crew are mustered in the mess room, Jason. I'm having to read them the riot act. Stok's refused to pay my men.'

Jason pursed his lips. 'How bad is it, sir?'

The Master did not reply. He nodded towards the door. 'Join the ship tomorrow, Jason, as early as you like.'

'But I've seen Hannah. She's in danger. We've got to get her out of her ship.'

'Keep your voice down,' Jones muttered. 'Karatz is outside. He's got me over a barrel. One thing at a time.'

'We've got one more day,' Jason whispered. 'Only another day to rescue her.' But Jones was shaking his head. He looked old now, very weary, hard-faced. Jason kept his eyes on the man who was deciding the order of priority between his ship, his crew, his daughter … a worrying revelation to the younger man.

'Join at 0900, Mercer,' he said, raising his voice. 'We'll be ready for you.' He strode to the door and wrenched it open. 'Goodnight.' He glared at the bull-necked Mate walking ostentatiously down the passageway. 'Come here, Mister. I've got something to say to you before I talk to the crew.' He turned his back on the scowling Swede and returned to his desk. Jason bumped into Karatz, who swore angrily while he glowered down at the visitor.

The Captain's door slammed. Race Observer Mercer was alone. He reached the upper deck, strolled past the deckhand and, preoccupied, walked down the gangplank. He would be glad to be sleeping in *Sherrilee* after all...

He was being caught up dramatically in this race by events beyond his wildest imaginings and fears. Things were whirling beyond his control: he was being pitchforked into making decisions which concerned others' lives. Though he resented this, he realized now that he cared deeply for Hannah Jones's safety. Caution, combined with a repressed anger, from now on would accompany him for the remainder of SACOR. This Race Observer had left his peace of mind ashore at Wellington. The voyage had been rough, so far; but, he wondered, was the passage ahead to be tougher yet?

CHAPTER FIFTEEN: A SHIP CONDEMNED

It was nine o'clock on the Thursday morning, 1 August, and already swelteringly hot. Jason moved into the shade of the awning and dumped his bag on the scorching teak deck. The petty officer at the head of *Windrose*'s gangway was a small, ferrety man of about thirty whom Jason did not recognize.

'Captain Jones, please. Jason Mercer: Race Observer for the Boston leg.'

The PO's eyes were close together and suspicious. 'The Master's ashore, sir.' The face was shut in, the voice wheedling. 'The First Mate's on board, sir. He'll see you, I'm sure, sir. Mr Karatz.'

'Who?' Then Jason recalled the face of the giant Swede.

'Karatz, sir. Karl Karatz: he joined at Rio, to relieve the First who copped it in Wellington.' He shook his head while he led the way aft. '"Killer-ship" they're calling this hooker. Stupid, sir. I joined *Windrose* when she got in here: I'm the new Bo'sun, Reg Posner.' A secretive smile floated across his face. 'No time yet to get things my way, sir.'

'What's *your* way, then?' Jason paused outside the wheelhouse door. 'You can tell me.' He was deliberately being dishonest now, scheming. 'It's my job to find out how things work out in all the ships.' He smiled for the first time at the shifty eyes, which instantly avoided his gaze.

'Cap'n's ashore, sir, rustling up the crew's pay. Ain't been paid yet and we've 'ad a spot of bovver.'

'So that's it. I'd heard something.'

'They're within their rights, sir. 'Alf of 'em were for jumping ship.' He winked slyly. 'There're two sides to a coin, ain't there, sir?' He selected Jason's cabin key from the board, then stood back to allow Jason to step over the coaming. 'Your cabin's right aft on the starboard side, sir.' He pointed down the passageway, dark after the sunlight.

When Jason reached the door of his cabin, a shadow etched itself from the gloom. 'Sails! What are you lurking about for? Good to see you again after Monte.' Sam Tyler waited for Jason to unlock the cabin door, then pushed his way inside; he slammed the door behind them. Jason could barely recognize him as the same petty officer whom he had got to know at Rio: his face was haggard, his eyes furtive. The Race Observer dropped his bag and slumped onto the bunk. 'Take the chair, Sails. Smoke if you like.'

Tyler shook his head. 'No time, sir.' He spoke hurriedly in a half-whisper, his head continually cocked, listening. '*You've* got to know what's going on. The Captain can't fight it all on his own, sir. The loyal men are windy…' He ended abruptly.

'Whom can you trust, Sam? The Mates?'

'Ben Bellew's not so bad, but he's weak: terrified of the First. The Third's as wet as a scrubber. Can't count on the Mates, but several of the ABs are loyal: Tregannon and Shiner Wright, the watch leading hands are dependable.'

'The Carpenter: Bert Hicks?'

'Chippy's all right, though he prefers to stay out of trouble. He keeps clear of the new Bo'sun, that creep, Posner. The hands are already calling him Tarzan, but he don't know it.'

'Another Stok man, like the Mate?'

'Yes, sir. You couldn't find a bigger bastard than that friggin' Swede: Karatz is as strong as an ox and don't mind using 'is mitts.'

'Doesn't anyone stand up to him?'

''Ow'd you like a broken jaw and a smashed nose?'

'The crew won't stand for it, surely? Witnesses and union backing?'

'Too many on 'is side, sir. Those six extra seamen who joined the day we got in: they're all Stok men, paid bullyboys.'

'How does Karatz manage to manipulate the crew?' Jason asked. 'They always respected Captain Jones.'

But Sam had shot to his feet when they both heard footsteps approaching along the corridor outside. There was a knock on the door, which was then pushed open. The impassive Chief Steward, immaculate in his white tunic and long trousers, poked his face through the gap as Sam flattened himself behind the door.

'Cap'n's compliments, sir. He'd like to see you in his cabin before he musters the crew.' The grey face cracked into a mechanical smile. 'Nice to have you on board for this leg of SACOR.' He quietly closed the cabin door.

They listened to his footsteps diminishing, then Sails slipped over, whispering over his shoulder, 'Remember, sir, we ain't met yet.' Then he was gone.

Jason opened his bag and searched for the comb. His hair (the grey flecks showed less in its fairness) was in need of a cut, he reckoned, as he twitched a smile at the image in the mirror. His face was too full and his solid frame, all six feet of it, looked in need of exercise. He would work off some of the flab during his leg in *Windrose*. Barnaby wouldn't object to his RO going aloft sometimes. He, Jason, would like to have a go at it, for he had never been out on the yardarm of a fully rigged ship. These blue eyes staring at him had grey shadows beneath them, half-moons of tiredness, caused surely by the pressures of the past twenty-four hours. He would broach the subject of

Hannah because she *had* to be extricated from her dangerous predicament before *Wandering Star* sailed tomorrow for the start of the Boston leg. He smoothed his hair, tried again to conceal its length behind his ears, then stepped out into the passageway.

A rectangle of sunlight shone at the far end, at the top of the ladder leading to the upper deck. A large, motionless figure was silhouetted against the glare and Jason knew instinctively whose it was: he had better be civil, whatever attitude Karatz took towards the ROs. Jason trotted up the ladder to the upper deck. The doorway was blocked by the Mate's back where he stood, feet astride and hands in shorts pockets, as he watched the hands trickling for'd to the foredeck.

'Excuse me…'

The man sniffed the sultry air, did not move.

Jason cleared his throat. 'Gangway, please…' No movement. He raised his voice. 'Gangway…' But now there was an edge to Jason's voice.

The lout could no longer ignore the request. He turned slowly but did not budge. Jason noted the black hair sprouting from his ears, bunching like moss on his chest where it showed beneath the unbuttoned shirt. The man's thighs were like oak trunks and covered with dark fuzz. Karatz glanced down at the pest who was daring to challenge him, his glowing black eyes, unusually dark for a Swede, flickering with amusement. '*Well?*'

'The Master's quarters?'

'And why d'you want him, for heaven's sake?'

The blasphemy needled Jason. 'I'm here for this leg. The Captain's waiting for me and I'm in a hurry.'

''kay, Mister.' Karatz stepped to the guardrail and spat into the smelly waters of the harbour. Jason felt the heat bouncing back at him from the deck which, even with a hose continually trickling water over it, was burning hot, sufficient to penetrate the soles of his shoes. He reached the wheelhouse as the first of the crew mustered aft: a morose, silent lot, where they gathered beneath the awning which was casting the only patch of shade. The Bo'sun, that insignificant Reg Posner, was fussing about like a wet hen while he chased the laggards. Jason entered the wheelhouse and knocked on the mahogany door in the after screen.

'What d'ye want?' Barnaby Jones growled, his voice unmistakable. 'Come in!'

Jason pushed open the door and stepped inside. The stocky figure in a white, open-necked shirt, shorts and white stockings was crouched over the central table, at his side the Purser, Henry Purl, a big man with a paunch and with pale, flabby cheeks. He was reading from the nominal list while Jones continued checking the pay packets. 'Who is it?' he asked, without looking upwards.

'Mercer, sir. Your RO for the Boston leg.'

Irritated, the Master paused in his counting to peer from beneath his bushy eyebrows. 'So it's you, this time? Make yourself comfortable. I've got to pay the crew and then I'll be with you.' The Captain resumed his work, but in that instant their eyes had met: unmistakable fear was reflected in that once untroubled, steady blue gaze.

The silent steward who had been hovering about the Captain's table during the hurried luncheon at last slipped from the cabin. Jones picked up his coffee and slumped into one of his two armchairs. He motioned Jason to the other and selected a cigar from the box on the bookshelf.

'Thank God, we can talk at last,' he murmured. 'Someone will be listening outside, so keep your voice down. Let me do the talking.'

Barnaby's gnarled fingers were trembling when he stroked the end of the cigar with the match flame. Clouds of blue, deliciously scented smoke hung above them, then spiralled beneath the slowly revolving, old-fashioned fan which he had brought with him from his last command, a bulker on the Bombay run. He drew in deeply, then exhaled in short gobs, like a fat carp in a still pool. In silence they watched the rings drifting to the deckhead, where they were dissipated by the fan blades to the whispering extraction of the ventilation trunking.

'Hannah: you've seen her?'

Jason nodded. 'Yesterday evening.'

'How is she?'

Jason bent forward, elbows on his knees, chin cupped in his hands. 'She's frightened,' he whispered. 'They might be holding her hostage.'

'Why?' But Barnaby answered his own question: 'To frighten me off, in case *Windrose* looks like winning?'

'Could be...'

'How is she?' the Master asked again, his eyes pleading for reassuring news.

'She's not herself. Difficult to explain. She disappeared and wouldn't let me talk. I'm sure she's terrified, sir, scared. I think they might have drugged her: there were bruises on her forearm. I'm certain of one thing...'

Barnaby leaned forward too, his face close to Jason's as he murmured, 'I've got to tell the police; get Gavin McBinney in Glasgow to put Interpol on the job.'

'From what I've gathered, they'd not bat an eyelid at killing her if you did that. She's certainly learned a lot about the Stok Mafia already.'

Jason wanted to reach out, lay his hand on the ageing seafarer's shoulder. Barnaby was slumped back in his chair, the fight apparently gone out of him. Then in the next few minutes, Jason learned why this proud, tough old seaman had reached the end of his resistance. The Captain whom every man-jack on board had respected and feared, was now a pathetic wreck.

On arriving in Belém on that Monday, 29 July, the purser went to the Global Sea Transport agents, the Banco Estado do Pará, to draw the crew's pay, only to be handed a confidential and personal letter from the President of GST, Stok, addressed to the Master of *Windrose*. The puzzled deputy bank manager shook his head wisely, spread wide his hands and regretfully stated that he could not authorize the cashing of *Windrose*'s pay cheque. It had been stopped.

It had taken time for Barnaby to absorb the contents of Stok's letter: Global Sea Transport considered that *Windrose* was under-manned; GST would provide enough money through the Brazilian bank to pay the extra men who had recently joined and who had been signed on by the company. The responsibility for payment of the remainder of the crew, Captain Jones's men, lay with the Master. If he could not fund and pay his crew, it was within the power of GST to dispense with the services of the Master and the unpaid crew who would have to find their own passage back to the UK. *Windrose* would then be withdrawn from the race and put up for sale. Further, if the Master refused to sign on the additional crew which was being flown out to Belém for the Boston leg, this failure would be considered a breach of contract; he would then be dismissed summarily, the First Mate, Captain Karl Karatz, taking over command.

Barnaby Jones leaned towards his desk and grabbed a slip of paper. 'Read that: these are some of the additional hands I've got to make up the deficiency in complement.'

Jason glanced at the sheet:

Fifth Engineer, additional: Ruth Biggs
Assistant Radio Officer: Rosemary Taylor
Assistant Purser: Hattie Ling
Assistant Steward: Penny Avery
Assistant Cook: Mary Wootton
Cadet Seaman: Gladys Thomson

Jason looked up, but failed to hide the astonishment in his eyes as he handed the sheet back to the man slumped in the chair.

'Wipe that stupid smirk off your face, for Pete's sake; I've never sailed with women as crew.'

'I'm sorry,' Jason muttered, 'really I am: but Stok is certainly doing all he can to oust you, isn't he?'

'*Women...*' Barnaby muttered. '*In my ship...*! They'll cause chaos! The man's a bloody lunatic!' He stared defiantly at Jason. 'Anyway, I've beaten the bastard by getting through to Gavin McBinney to fix a banker's draft. That's why I wasn't here when you arrived. I'm paying my men as soon as they're mustered.'

'Isn't your Ocean Shipping Line still operating then, sir?'

'No. Stok gobbled it up. But Gavin has salted funds away in our subsidiary. There's not enough money, though, to pay them after Boston.'

'You know you've got trouble 'tween decks, Captain?' Jason did not enjoy posing the question. Barnaby seemed to have diminished, was trying to hide himself in his voluminous chair.

'Who told you that? You've only been on board a few moments.'

'Sam Tyler, sir. Perhaps he was exaggerating, but he seemed scared.'

'Sails is one of the few I can trust now. The Mate and his cronies have worked fast. Even if I do pay the hands, I still don't know whether they'll work the ship.'

'What d'you mean?' Jason leaned forward even further, as Barnaby dropped his voice. 'Mutiny?'

'I've hoisted the Blue Peter: the start begins at 1000 tomorrow. I'm slipping at 1800 this evening and moving out to the anchorage. No leave tonight. I need a fit crew.'

'That's why the hands are seething, then? They've been waiting to spend their pay in Belém?'

Barnaby nodded. 'I'll play it by ear when I pay them. I won't budge on this. I sail at six.'

Jason kept silent, recognizing how vital the decision was, if the Master still wished to command the ship. 'And your Mate, Karatz, sir?'

'Making the most of my discomfiture. He's a clever swine: keeps just on the right side without being mutinous. He's stirring things behind my back — "dumb insolence", the army call it. And I can't sack him. Not yet.'

Jones seemed sunk in deep despair. There was a long silence, and then he said quietly, 'I'll chuck it in after Boston. I don't suppose *Windrose* is in the running anyway.'

'Tomorrow's controlled start will give us some idea, won't it?' Jason asked.

'Crossing the starting-line at fifteen-minute intervals, in reverse order of results so far,' Barnaby said glumly. 'That's why I'm sailing tonight. We're bound to be near the last, so will be among the first to start. Right?' Barnaby's listless eyes met Jason's. 'Hannah's more important to me than fighting Stok's damnable Mafia,' he muttered. 'I'll withdraw *Windrose* at Boston. I'll put the police on to snatching Hannah from that Randy Buckle's clutches. Should have done it earlier...' He was mumbling to himself, in utter despair. 'And I've lost a man aloft. They murdered Tom Hawkins... God! How was I to know?'

'That's exactly what Stok has planned: he's driving you to retire. You're only playing into his hands if you give up.' It was difficult for Jason to control his voice. 'Can't you see? Why not get the police now?'

'*For God's sake, dry up!*' Those tired eyes flashed with their natural fire. 'She's *my* only daughter, not yours.'

'She'd hate it, if you chuck your hand in. She's longing for you to win.'

Jones stiffened, his chin jutting. 'You mean that? Really think that?'

'I do. You've always been a fighter. "Give 'em all hell" was what you'd normally tell me.' The muffled conversation ended in a long, painful silence.

The Master dragged himself slowly from his chair. He stuffed his hands into his pockets, then went to the scuttle on the sunny side. In the stillness, Jason could hear the distant cries of the market traders; from seaward came the toot-toot of a tug. 'And what about Hannah?' Jones spat the question, fighting at last. 'I'll get on to the Consul. Come and see me after I've talked to the crew.'

And as Jason saw the broad back bracing itself, there was an imperious knocking on the door. It flung open to be filled by the towering bulk of Karatz.

'The hands are mustered,' he reported gruffly. 'It's hot on deck.'

Jones said nothing. As he walked slowly forward to stand in front of his Mate, he withdrew his hands from his pockets. His eyes were blazing as he fixed the Swede with an unflinching stare. 'Mister,' he said deliberately. 'You'll call your Master, "sir". And if there's any more of your insolence, I'll put you ashore.' The two men gazed at each other for what seemed an eternity. Neither moved.

'Understand, Mister?' Jones spoke softly.

Karatz hesitated a further second, then lowered his eyes. He stood back, holding open the door. 'Yes. The hands are ready … *sir*.' There was mockery in his voice, but his bravado seemed false to Jason. 'Nine men have broken ship.'

Barnaby picked up his cap, set it squarely on his head, stomped from the cabin. Jason would not have relished being in the shoes of anyone fool enough to challenge the Captain's authority at this instant: there were squalls ahead. Captain Jones was Master of his ship again, but for how long was anybody's guess. Jason hoped that race fever still gripped *Windrose*'s company, a bonus which surely would help the Master when confronting his men. But, if so, was this engendered ship's spirit strong enough to endure whatever lay ahead?

CHAPTER SIXTEEN: A SHIP DIVIDED

At three o'clock on Friday, 2 August, *Niger*, with her twin wing sails drawing, trundled across the starting line in Guarajá Bay, a gargantuan bulker but whose Walker Wingsails' efficiency was placing her ninth so far in the race. She was followed in eighth place by *Pollux*, the 27,000-ton West German, four-masted dynaship whose snowy sails soared to impossible heights; and then, as Jason watched the great ship heeling to the breeze, he saw a string of flags peeling to the truck of the mast on the tower of the Port Control at the Harbour Master's building: the four signal letters of *Windrose!*, *GQJX*, the identification flags for which everyone in the barque had been straining their eyes for so long.

'Bear away,' Captain Jones ordered quietly. 'Set all plain sail, Mister Mate.'

For the past two hours *Windrose* had been gilling about the bay under only main lower topsail, jib, fore staysail and spanker.

Karl Karatz stood at the rail, megaphone to his lips, barking his orders. The lower lifts had been set up taut and all the hoisting yards were on their lifts. The two hands on each yard had already overhauled the buntlines.

'Sheet home fore lower topsail.' The order boomed for'd and was repeated through the upper deck loudspeakers. And as the Quartermaster bore away, sail after sail began to break from the yards. The main topsail being already set, first the fore lower topsail, then the jigger, spanker and lastly the after-mast sails were sheeted home. It fascinated Jason to watch the well-used canvas billowing outwards, to set like banks of cumulus as the great ship gathered way under all plain sail. Next the topgallants and royals were broken out, then the huge courses which just cleared the port bulwarks when she listed to her starboard tack. The staysails, outer and inner jibs rattled up the forestays until the bowsprit was festooned with curving triangular canvas. She was the most beautiful ship Jason had ever seen: there was even a smirk of satisfaction on Karatz's face when finally he reported to his Captain that all sail was set.

By now, *Windrose* was almost clear of the bay, *Pollux*, with her bulk coal products, being over three miles ahead. *Niger* was already hull-down to the northward; the horizon line was studded with the fast-disappearing smudges and mastheads of those ships who had started first: up ahead were the tail-end Charlies led by *Ocean Kite*; then *Sao Isabel*; then *Wicher*, *Sea Falcon*, *Storm Petrel*, *Stella Venus* and *Yankee Flyer*, in that order. Barnaby Jones passed over his binoculars to Jason.

'*Pollux* is too close to us in the race order for comfort, Mr Mercer. *Windrose* is seventh and only six points separate us: *Pollux* will probably beat us on loading: she's a taut ship.'

Jason held the glasses to his eyes, and the pyramidal, rigid white sails sprang into focus.

Captain Jones ruminated at Jason's elbow. 'One day they could revolutionize sea transport,' Barnaby murmured. 'But there are a lot of snags to cure first. Aircraft designers tried out their sails and revolving masts in the Hamburg wind tunnels and got excellent results. Dynaships have no curved yards, their rigid sails having aerofoil profiles; the yards are fixed to the masts which revolve on a training pad fitted to the upper deck and braced below on the main deck.'

'The stresses must be enormous on the mast,' Jason remarked. *Pollux* seemed to be unreal, creaming along with a gentle list, spray cascading from her sharp bows, her decks apparently deserted. She was taking a deal of catching and with this breeze seemed to have the legs on *Windrose*.

'Theoretically, the aircraft engineers are on to a good thing,' Jones said. 'But in practice they can't compete with what every Cape Horner learned the hard way: the wind's angle of attack across the deck is very different from that aloft, against the royals.'

Jason lowered the glasses, enthralled by what he was learning of this new maritime technology.

'Supposing you've got a wind speed at sea level of fifteen knots,' Jones said. 'At a height of 25 metres, you can add 10%; at 45 metres, 33%.'

'At *Pollux*'s masthead?' Jason asked.

'Could be sea level wind speed plus 60%. It'll be blowing hard in the royals.'

'And the apparent wind,' Jason asked. 'Does that alter with height?'

'It certainly does: the angle of attack can be the required fifteen degrees at deck level. Two hundred feet up, the angle has slanted aft and can be at about forty degrees, so the royals and topgallants are only pushing the ship sideways. You can't alter the angle of the individual yards in a dynaship because they are fixed to the mast. You lose 40% of the driving power, because you can't trim a dynaship's upper sails.'

'You're biased,' Jason laughed. 'Look at *Pollux*: she's going well and looks good.' Barnaby smiled briefly: they shared the gift of a true seaman's eye.

'There's another thing,' Jones added quietly, when Karatz approached them. 'The dynaship has one enormous failing which she cannot rectify: her performance to windward is dependent entirely upon the aerofoil form of her sails. The distance between each yard is constant, so a taut and higher leach is vital to the ship's performance. If she has a slack leach, there's no aerofoil effect: she'll wear round to windward. No one has yet succeeded in making an unstretchable sail, so her leaches are going to stretch.'

'Can't they take up the slack?' Jason asked.

'No way: distances between the yards are constant, as I told you. In no time at all, she'll have a lot of dirty linen hanging up there which will be very inefficient. And have you considered what happens if one of their sails burst: how do you go aloft to sort things out?'

'Inside the mast,' Jason said.

'You can't do much from inside there. Because there's no rigging, if a sail blows out, it will either wreck the yard above and below; or, when you push the button and wind up the loose-flying fabric, it will jam everything inside the mast. Imagine the shambles during a gale! You would have no way of clearing it and what could be worse than that?'

'You'd lose the ship,' Jason said.

'There are plenty more design features which I'd hate to handle.' Barnaby jerked his head towards the German dynaship. 'She's the first to have made it. All the other previous dynaship companies went bankrupt.'

'You don't approve of them, *nein*?' Karatz butted in, staring at Jason. 'But she's showing us her pair of boots, as you English say, *ja*?'

'Heels,' Jason said. 'Pair of…'

'Set the watch,' Jones ordered. 'Get your soup, Mister,' he told the Mate. 'I'll take her until you get back for the twelve-to-four.'

Karatz was watching his Captain from the corners of his eyes. He grunted and, without saluting, rolled from the bridge.

He went up to an older-looking seaman on the working deck and tapped him on the shoulder.

'Shiner Wright: he's the watch leader,' Jones said, pointing out the stocky fair-haired able seaman. 'Works the Mate's watch, but joined the ship for her first trip.'

They watched in silence while the two men seemed to lapse into heated argument. Finally the seaman shrugged his shoulders and continued coiling a rope while his men swarmed down from aloft.

'A good hand?' Jason asked.

The Master nodded. 'One of my best: he and the starboard watch leader, Tregannon, hate the Mate's guts.'

Karatz was stomping aft towards the door in the after screen, and even from the wheelhouse his filthy language was audible. And as Jason turned to go below, he spotted the outline of several heads pressed against the side of the doorway in the fo'c'sle head. Then they disappeared, one by one.

It was shortly after 2000, when the low coastline had vanished in a shimmering heat haze, that the wind died to leave only a rare catspaw. It was too hot below for comfort, even after twilight, and everyone except the Captain was up top to savour the cool of the night. The sails were hanging like washing from every yard, when Barnaby Jones came on deck.

'The Doldrums,' he muttered. 'Tell the Chief to let me have the engine.'

The soft accent of the Glaswegian Engineer droned from the moon's long shadow abaft the wheelhouse. 'Aye. And how long will ye be needing it, Cap'n?'

'A day or two,' Jones said. 'The Doldrums are reduced at this time of year.' He turned to the Mate: 'Furl everything, Mister, but leave the spanker.'

While Karatz searched for his megaphone, Jason, to satisfy a latent ambition, asked the Captain for permission to go aloft with the watch.

'Get the leading hand to show you the ropes, Mercer.' He turned to Karatz. 'Who is he, Mister?'

'Tregannon, Cap'n. Starboard watch is on deck.' The Mate's black eyebrows were knotted in disapproval. 'Aren't you risking disqualification if the Race Observer goes aloft?'

Jones ignored the question and told Jason to get on with it. 'But read my orders before you go up,' he added, casting an eye aloft. 'Her mast caps are fifty-six metres above her keel.' While the Mate mustered both watches, Jason entered the wheelhouse to read the orders mounted on the after bulkhead. His life was to depend on these rules.

1. Avoid showing off.

2. A man has four points of contact: two feet and two hands. Always have three of them in firm contact with the rig. Never use any part of the running rigging for climbing, or for support: it may come slack and throw you off the mast or yard…

3. When climbing up the ratlines, always use the shrouds: ratlines are light and can carry away. Always climb one ratline at a time.

4. When laying out on a yard, use the safety jackstay. Never trust a gasket, bight of sail, clew line or buntline. Always use the arm beckets when furling sail.

5. Never stand on a yard, unless ordered under special circumstances. When you do so, remember what will happen if the sail fills with wind. Make certain you are gripping a part of the standing rigging.

The deck beneath Jason's feet trembled, then vibrated steadily while the engine worked up to its economical revs. By the time the sails were furled, the Chief would be ready to throw in the clutches. Jason finished reading the final two rules:

6. Always go aloft on the weather shrouds.
7. Always work on the weather side of the bowsprit.

Then he walked outside to where Tregannon was waiting for him.

'The hands are aloft, sir. We'll take the foremast and I'll be behind you, but first you better get into more suitable boots.'

It was the Saturday, a day later, and an hour after Jason had turned in for the night that the thumping of the engine died away. From his bunk right aft, the RO heard the pounding above him and the commands of the Mate as the sails were set again. Jason could not sleep while listening to the sequence: setting lower and upper topsails, topgallants and royals, courses and then the headsails. Barnaby was wasting no time, not a drop of fuel. And in the blessed peace of sailing once again, Jason at last found sleep; tomorrow was another day, tomorrow was Sunday, 4 August ... and *Windrose* had at last prised herself from the Doldrums. Not for nothing were these windless, oceanic deserts called the Horse Latitudes in bygone days: ships carrying horses as cargo often had to ditch the animals to conserve drinking water. *Windrose* had been lucky so far dodging the *pamperos* off the Plate and enjoying superb sailing ever since. The Doldrums were astern and only the Sargasso lay ahead between her and Boston ... and then the final race home.

As Jason drowsily dropped into sleep, tired after going round the ship all day and making up his records, he wondered which ship he would pick up for the final leg home to the finishing line. And would Hannah be there in England, welcoming *Windrose* home? Her father had tried to organize the Belém consul to arrange for her to disembark, so she might be flying home by now: a relief to Jason, though it would be a disappointment for Hannah, who had been so keen to take part in the great race.

CHAPTER SEVENTEEN: '…CAME AWAY IN ME 'AND, SIR.'

Sunday dawned bright with a crystal-clear sky to the eastward and a fitful breeze soughing in a muggy, sweltering atmosphere. Before *Windrose* crossed the Equator, Captain Jones held a short Sunday service of prayers and readings from the gospels, a ritual which he had always conducted whilst in command. Jason savoured this moment of peace. He was surprised by the number of men who attended in the shade of the jigger course, men whose lives depended on their own stamina and the skill of this man, their stocky skipper, standing feet astride, the breeze blowing through his grizzled hair, the battered prayer book in his hands. It was an interlude which under happier circumstances drew men together: the RO felt an affinity with the man who had the guts to give a lead in what he believed.

Jason found his thoughts wandering to Hannah Jones who *might* still be virtually a prisoner in that schooner somewhere astern of *Windrose*: *Sherrilee* had crossed the starting line next after *Windrose*, then *Red Star*, *Cousteau* and, in fifth place, *Wandering Star*. *Rêve de l'Avenir* had been the penultimate across the line in second place, with *Techno Phanta* starting last, the 17,600-ton horizontal windmill ship of Stok's contingent. She was therefore the SACOR leader at the moment.

What were Barnaby's feelings now? He *seemed* callously stoical about the dangerous situation; Buckle was a menace and if he was drugging Hannah, what on earth could Jones do, if she insisted on remaining in *Wandering Star*? There had been an unguarded moment earlier this morning, when Jason had come upon the Master standing by himself on the port corner of the poop deck: he was staring aft, his eyes sweeping the horizon. He had not noticed his RO's approach and when finally he turned, the despair in those clear blue eyes would not be forgotten by Jason for a long time.

Jason pulled himself together as Captain Jones drew the service to a close with the prayer:

'So when they cry unto the Lord in their trouble: He delivered them out of their distress.
For He maketh the storm to cease: so that the waves thereof are still.
Then are they glad, because they are at rest: and so He bringeth them unto the haven where they would be...'

He ended with the general blessing and after the gathering had dispersed, Tregannon came up to the RO. 'How d'you enjoy your first climb aloft, sir?'

'Enjoy is hardly the right word,' Jason laughed. 'I was scared stiff.'

'You soon get used to it,' the leading seaman replied. 'It's when you're cold and worn out that it's dicey. Next time, you can work out on the yardarm: I'll be right behind you.' He saluted and walked for'd, deliberately choosing the starboard side: the Mate was haranguing a couple of men on the port, one of them being Posner, the Bo'sun.

And so that Sunday, 4 August, wore slowly on, an uneasy atmosphere hanging over them all, like a gathering summer storm. Before turning in, Jason went into the charthouse to check the ship's position: by Satnav, the barque was already 495 miles due east of Bridgetown. Two mastheads had come up over the horizon shortly before dusk, but no lights were sighted throughout the night.

Jason was up early on that Monday, 5 August. Barbados was well astern on their port quarter; and the Leewards 480 miles to the westward of Antigua, with its English Harbour, Nelson's base, being still a memory from Jason's cadet days when he first went to sea in the Fyffe banana boats. But the West Indies were now dependent upon tourism, and this was changing everything.

As he stood by himself watching the blood-red dawn rearing along the horizon, he shivered in the humid morning: there was a clamminess in the air, a brooding heaviness which hung low upon the sea like a blanket. The sun was concealed behind a shroud of misty haze, where it climbed into the steely sky. He sensed an unease he could not explain; he was depressed perhaps by the bloody-mindedness festering in this once-happy ship. It was a quarter to six when he went below to clean up. He would like to listen to the SACOR news on the radio at breakfast: he'd like to know the 0800 position of the other competitors: this Boston leg was the most important of them all, before the final run home across the Atlantic. The Captain's watch was well into the Monday forenoon, when the Bo'sun sent aloft the main lower topgallant sail for bending on to the yard. Tregannon was down on deck and supervising the hands manning the electric capstan which was to haul away on the buntlines for hoisting the head of the sail up to the yard. Jason, who, with the Master's dispensation, was now accepted as an honorary member of the starboard watch, was sitting astride the port and leeward yardarm of the main upper topgallant yard; he was waiting to receive and reeve the earing so that the head of the sail could be hauled out to the yardarm.

He was becoming less terrified of this shattering work which forced every sinew to respond to the reflexes induced by fear. Here, hanging out one hundred and sixty feet above the ocean where the white crests broke like snowflakes upon the long swell's blue mountain sides, he knew he was suspended between life and death. Only his muscles and mental reactions separated him from hurtling to a messy extinction: he could understand now why seafarers tended to regard landlubbers with condescension. Below, he could see the deckhands backing up the gantlines, as others manned the clewlines while they waited for the Bo'sun's and Tregannon's orders.

'...*Haul away*!' The command floated upwards against the roar of the wind battering the canvas of the royals above. Then Jason saw the great sail crawling upwards towards the waiting men lying out along the yard. And as the ship leaned to the wind and her yards canted skywards to windward, he watched her bowsprit heaving above the horizon line: a long spear with its jibs curving to the breeze, like the convoluted leaves of arum lilies. From up here, the horizon was fifteen miles distant, but there was nothing, nothing but an endless circle of graduating blues and purples where the sunlight and cloud shadows drifted across the surface of the ocean. Yesterday, the ship had excited a school of dolphins: a glorious sight they made as they gambolled on each bow, curving in unison, arched like leaping seahorses clearing their jumps. Today he could pick out the rainbow-hued flying fish, shooting from their watery world to glide for hundreds of yards in crescent flight before splashing back to their own element. It was good to be alive, Jason felt, up here and divorced from the futility of human behaviour.

There was a sudden cry from the deck below, a shout of fear and anger. Peering upwards was a sea of minuscule faces.

Posner, the Bo'sun, was shaking his fist upwards ludicrously. Tregannon was bending down and prising something from the teak. He jerked straight, standing erect. He was holding a marline spike in his hand. It had pierced the deck within a foot of him, between him and the capstan, but well clear of the others.

'Who dropped this spike?'

Posner was screaming upwards against the booming of the wind in the sails. Jason glanced along the yard: the other eight hands were staring downwards, callous and silent. Most of these were Stok's men. They hated Tregannon and despised the loyal men. A few seconds passed while they glanced at each other, and then they turned again to bending on the sail. Twenty minutes later, they were ordered on deck. The Mate was standing feet astride, arms akimbo, waiting silently for them: there was an inscrutable leer on his upturned face.

CHAPTER EIGHTEEN: HELGA

After a painfully silent dinner, Jason went up to the poop deck before turning in on that sultry Monday night of 5 August. It was mysteriously beautiful up here, where he stood watching the phosphorescence bubbling astern in *Windrose*'s wake. There were only a few others there, inevitably those Don Juans determined to steal a march chatting up the off-watch members of the new women crew; others were laughing softly as they puffed at their strong Brazilian cigarillos.

Still shocked by this afternoon's attempted murder, Jason needed solitude, for he was reluctant to meddle in this unhappy ship's affairs. Jason was forced to keep himself apart, if he was to be available should Captain Jones call upon him for help. It was no surprise that the investigation which the Mate had carried out failed to draw a conclusion, or to accuse any of the eight seamen who had been aloft with Jason on that yard. Karatz had included the Race Observer in his cross-questioning and at one moment had even hinted that Jason was suspect. The enquiry was farcical and embarrassing. It was miraculous that Tregannon had stepped aside when the spike had skewered the deck.

Jason lit a cigar. The breeze sighed in the rigging, while the mastheads swayed against the myriads of twinkling stars: the night was fine but already less tropical, with high cirrus tiptoeing in slowly from the west. The Southern Cross disappeared two nights ago, on that first night out of Belém, and *Windrose* should be picking up the Pole Star on any night now. It was good to be plying northern latitudes again, under familiar night skies and stars: there was Aldebaran and Dubhe, and it was good also to pick up the Pleiades again. He was keen to get home to England and to find a ship with a stable shipping company again. Things were bucking up after the catastrophic early 1980s, when politicians realized at last that Britain's existence depended upon its maritime trade and merchant fleet.

'Evening, Mercer,' Barnaby's quiet voice greeted from the shadows. 'Airless, isn't it?'

'It's muggy below. I'm snatching a breather before taking today's final readings.'

'Your cabin is above the screw, I'm afraid. Does it worry you?'

'Only when the engines are running.'

'Tell me if I forget to feather the propeller when sailing,' Barnaby said. 'Have you seen the eight o'clock Seafax?'

'There's quite a "low" building to the north of the Cape Verdes,' Jason replied. 'I'm glad it's so far away.'

'We'll keep an eye on it, though.' Barnaby paused before adding, 'I've often wondered why Stok bamboozled the SACOR planners to bring us through these parts at this time of the year.' He laughed shortly. 'I'm beginning to see why.'

'The hurricane season?' Jason asked.

'If our SACOR runs into one of those, the men should be sorted out from the boys.'

'Stok has as much to lose as anyone.'

'He entered more starters than anyone else. He's put his shirt on winning this SACOR.'

'And destroying you and *Windrose* in the process.'

'Even resorting to murder,' Barnaby muttered as a shadow spilled across the deck. He raised his voice. 'Tell the Mates to keep an eye on the glass, Mister. Call me if there's any change.'

Karatz was standing underneath the boom of the spanker; he pulled at the cigarette which he gripped in the vee of his middle fingers as the smoke spiralled to leeward. The glow of the wheelhouse lighting shone on the Quartermaster, who was seated on the helmsman's chair. The ship was reaching on the starboard tack, the wind south-east, Force 5. It was invigorating sailing with the barque making eighteen knots, the sea hissing along her sides. Still wet from the last shower, the deck glistened in the moonlight: the rain had begun in the afternoon, warm, solid sheets of it, flattening the surface of the sea. The showers were now more frequent as forked-lightning slashed across the eastern skyline. Jason stayed on deck until he reached the stub of his cigar. The lightning had altered to the flickering chain flashes of an inaudible storm below the horizon away to the east.

The Captain bade a general 'goodnight' and disappeared inside the wheelhouse. 'Watch the glass,' he snapped once again to the officer of the watch, before retiring to his sea cabin.

It was *Windrose*'s unusual rolling which awoke Jason at 0530. Slipping into his sea-going gear, he hauled himself up to the bridge where the Captain, Mate and Bo'sun were congregated. The ship was lurching from a sea whipped up by north-easterly squalls of over 50 knots as registered by the anemometer. During the four-to-eight, the Mate's watch, the Master had taken in the royals and upper topgallants; the watch was now aloft, putting on the gaskets, and *Windrose* was still making eighteen knots.

Down below, everything moveable had been placed on deck and lashed where it could fall no further. With the spanker and topsail off, the ship was steering well, her fore topmast staysail and inner jib flying like pocket handkerchiefs from the denuded bowsprit. Jason had never sailed in a big barque and was fascinated by her sensitivity in the hands of a skilled helmsman and experienced master. He entered the wheelhouse where the Second Mate, Ben Bellew, was poring over the chart and pricking off distances on the North Atlantic chart.

'We've received the eight o'clock Weatherfax, Jason,' Ben announced. 'The States' Weather Bureau had just given this "low" an official name: "Helga".' Bellew stood back and pointed to the depression's position. 'There's its centre, eighty miles east of us and travelling north-west: a potential hurricane.'

Bellew had marked the storm's track in red on the chart: from *Windrose*'s course and daily noon positions, it looked as if by tomorrow the storm would be still converging on a collision course. The Captain was standing on the bridge wing and staring at the rig, then at the darkening, eastern horizon. Jason decided to go below and swallow some food before the motion became too wretched. He moved out to the lee side to sniff the air, to listen to the booming of the wind in the rigging. Along the eastern horizon the sky was slashed with blood-red streaks; from the westward and high up, a silvery-grey film of mare's-tail cirrus was creeping across the sky.

The day wore on, the barometer falling slowly, the weather deteriorating during each watch. *Windrose* crossed the Tropic of Cancer at 1115 and during the late afternoon began to cleave through bands of surface weed, the dustbin of the Sargasso Sea. It was a satisfactory sight, proof that she was making good progress, and something to raise the spirits of this sullen company. Even some of the female crew were on deck to take the air.

Never had Jason served in such tense conditions and, like everyone on board at the moment, he would be thankful to quit as soon as he could. It was like sitting on top of a fuse spluttering towards a detonator. There was only one unknown factor: when would the whole lot blow up? Karatz's enquiry had produced no tangible evidence, in spite of the preponderance of new men. Now even the fo'c'sle hands were divided into two factions: those anti- and those pro-skipper.

'Sails', Sam Tyler, had bumped into Jason on the upper deck when the hands were securing for heavy weather. He had muttered that the situation was explosive ... and then, at midday, when Bellew was taking his noon sight, Jason saw that ominous phenomenon, a halo encircling the sun; then a darkening sky and a sinister, yellow light suffusing most of the south and western horizon. At dusk, a big swell came rolling in from the east. The edges of the clouds were distinctly shaped and at sunset the western horizon glowed a vivid gold, shot with crimson streaks.

'It's going to blow,' Bellew muttered. 'I've seen it only once like this before: in the China Sea, before a typhoon.' He added with a short laugh, 'And I wasn't in a sailing ship, then.' He moved over to read the barometer swinging in its gimbals. '29.37,' he murmured, 'and still falling.'

At 2230 the Captain talked to his ship's company over the broadcast system. He was taking *Windrose* east of Bermuda as fast as he could, to pass ahead of the advancing low. By doing so, he would try to avoid being caught in the dangerous quadrant, even if Helga was to recurve and swing round. Jones then had 'All Hands': with the rising wind booming in the rigging, he took in all topgallants and all upper topsails. He hauled *Windrose* round to the port tack and steadied her on a heading of 100°. Not before he was satisfied, did he send the hands below. Everyone should get in as much sleep as he could: if this low developed into a hurricane, the ship's survival could in the end depend entirely upon her crew's stamina.

At 0400, in spite of it being the Mate's watch, Jason climbed up to the bridge. He had had enough of being hurled from one side of his bunk to the other. He had dossed down on the deck and propped himself against the bunk board with his chair, but even that had been useless.

The barometer was down to 29.30 and now dropping fast. The Old Man was propped in his corner, while Karatz prowled from one side of the rolling wheelhouse to the other. *Windrose*, under only two headsails and four lower topsails, was close-hauled and thrashing into the safe semi-circle of the storm: up to this point, no one had cared to use the dreaded word 'hurricane'.

Then, just before 0500, the dark, scudding clouds burst. Even during his days in the East, Jason had never seen such a downpour of rain: it was as if the plug had been taken out of some heavenly bath. Sheets of rain were bouncing onto the waves. A ghostly vapour hung in a mist above the boiling, hissing surface of the sea, when the advancing squall, roaring like the Edinburgh express, hit the ship from an unexpected quarter. And as *Windrose* shuddered and heeled to the blow, Jason heard the Quartermaster yelling that his steering had gone.

'Steering in hand,' the Master barked. 'Open the bypasses.' The changeover was carried out without fuss and seconds later the two, big, six-feet-diameter wheels right aft were manned. *Windrose* came slowly back to her new course of 330°. A sea crashed on board, smothering her until her bulwarks were under water. Jason heard a splintering crash, glimpsed the port boat being wrenched from its davits aft of the wheelhouse. *Another one like that,* he thought, *and I won't give much of a chance for the deckhouse.*

The Captain must have thought the same, for at that moment he yelled to the Mate, 'Run with the wind on the starboard quarter, Mister.'

Another squall smote the ship. There was a noise like thunder, the ship trembled and the inner jib flogged off to leeward in tatters. 'Stand by the fore lee braces,' Jones barked.

Jason watched the men nipping up on the lifelines as the seas crashed on board, until at last the braces were manned, with Tregannon staring towards the Mate and waiting for orders.

'Starboard the helm,' the Master yelled. 'Bring her up.'

The sails jerked as the braces were slacked … and then there was a sound like a salvo of cannon. Bits of canvas flew away in the wind as the lower main topsail blew out. *Windrose* was struck by a sledge-hammer blow. She heeled suddenly to port and was held there by the Herculean wind. She lay there for an interminable time, her lee rail under water and the sea swirling about her containers.

'Lost steerage way,' the frightened voice of the Quartermaster yelled, 'she don't answer, sir.'

The Captain crossed to the engine-room telephone. But as he yelled for maximum power, he was hurled off his feet by another monstrous sea which rampaged from the dark horizon boiling ahead.

'She's going!' someone yelled. *'My God…'*

Windrose hung there, her lee rail submerged, her hull still making way through the water. The noise was devastating and even Jones's commands, shouted at the top of his voice, while he staggered to his feet, were carried away on the wind. Bodies in the wheelhouse were huddled where they had fallen until, imperceptibly, *Windrose* began to shake herself from the sea's mortal embrace. Slowly she began to right herself, then, taking everyone by surprise, she catapulted upwards. There was an ear-splitting *crack!* Jason spun round towards the noise, which had come from the well deck.

The after container on the starboard side had ripped its securing chains from the deck, the eye-bolts flying about in the wind like bullets. And as the ship heaved, the after end of the box began slithering across the flooded deck. It swung, all forty tons of it, with an almighty *crash!* against the partners of the jigger mast.

'My God!' Bellew shouted. 'The whole lot'll come down, Mercer.'

There was no need to state the obvious: another blow like that, which had caused the hull to shudder from stem to stern, would carry away the mast, bringing down the others, one after the other, until *Windrose* was a foundering wreck.

'Watch the ship,' Barnaby yelled to his Mate. 'Run down wind.' He glanced at Mercer and the other two Mates, then hurled open the lee door of the wheelhouse.

It was raging outside, the wind tearing at Jason's anorak as he followed the Master down the ladder to the well deck. With the chains flailing murderously about their heads and up to their waists in water, they wrestled with the two-and-a-half-inch wire reeled up in the starboard corner. They overhauled it, Jones working the brake while Bellew and Jason floundered, half on their knees and half-upright, struggling to pass the eye of the wire through a bight in the after lashing. Then, sprawling on their stomachs, they sheltered behind the mast while the Third Mate, Tony Fisher, slammed in the clutch of the electric motor. The winch whined, the wire bounced, shivered as it came up all-standing ... and the box was held in its crazy slide.

'Nip it when I come up,' Barnaby shouted and, without waiting, he threw off the turns. Jason and Bellew hurled themselves at the bight, flung the slack over the bitts and hung on, backing it up until they could double up.

The box jerked again, shuddered, held firm. They doubled up again. Then they scrambled back to the wheelhouse and slammed shut the door behind them.

'That should hold,' Jones called out. 'Now, Mister, what's your heading?'

The ship scudded twice around the horizon during those twenty-nine hours. The barometer dropped to 29.05 but even while *Windrose* was running under bare poles, the seas were breaking bodily over her. It was the longest night that Jason had ever known, a night of furious wind and seas. At 0500 on the morning of Thursday, 8 August, Bellew reported twenty-five fathoms on the echo sounder.

To everyone except Captain Jones this shocking announcement meant the end; but Tregannon's watch battled to let go both anchors which held in 16 fathoms; a miracle, for *Windrose* could be on the edge of the reefs. Bermuda's 365 coral islands must be under *Windrose*'s lee.

Nothing could be seen when dawn broke, nothing but a furious cauldron of seas boiling and leaping on the edge of the murderous coral reefs. The thunderous booming was unnerving: at any second the screech of rending metal plating could overwhelm all other sounds.

The Captain ordered an oil bag to be streamed over the bow and while this was being rigged, the Chief also trickled oil through two of the heads' outlets. The effect was dramatic, the oil slick to windward immediately calming down the seas which no longer broke on board in fury. Then, at half-past nine, the cables parted, as the eye of the hurricane passed over. In the awesome calm, Jones himself bullied and cajoled the crew, driving them to efforts of which they never knew they were capable.

The barometer was touching 28.90. In the wheelhouse, Karatz was a beaten hulk, speechless, his eyes wild with terror, his lips trembling. Jones, jumping down to the well deck to be with Sails and Tregannon, cursed his crew, driving them to feats of endurance and courage beyond belief. They managed to set the fore top mast staysail seconds before the wind struck *Windrose* like a hammer from the starboard side. The blow shook the length of her, driving her bodily sideways. And, as the sun broke fitfully through, pale ochre and gleaming in the scud, they spotted the low-lying islands of Somerset and Ireland, mauve smudges above the boiling seas. The reefs greedily waiting to rip the bottom out of the ship could not have been more than a mile away.

Then *Windrose*, for the next eight hours under the staysail, was blown north-westwards again; but now she was under control and gaining freeboard as the pumps sucked at her bilges. The Chief succeeded in keeping them running and by 2100 of that night, *Windrose* was riding out the last of the hurricane. The barometer rose to 29.40; and at 2300, the wind shifted to south-east again, moderating to a Force 9 gale. She had scudded round the compass once more, but with Jones's leadership and clear-headed thinking, the barque had survived.

By Friday, 9 August, the hurricane had swept north-westward to leave a mountainous swell behind it. Helga swung north, then north-east, leaving New York only four hundred miles to the west. The complex depression then turned north and, dissipating into a succession of gales off Iceland and the Western Approaches, finally blew itself out.

During all that Friday, 9 August, Jones nursed his ship northwards while his crew slept. The watches and daymen gradually set *Windrose*'s canvas again until, by Saturday, she was under full sail again. And throughout that tragic day, the news of Helga's victims filtered through the radio. By the time that Cape Cod appeared on the starboard bow through the murk, it had been confirmed that *Rêve de l'Avenir* had been sunk; *Techno Phanta* and *Pollux* had vanished without trace; and that the US coastguard and aircraft were carrying out a massive search for survivors. As *Windrose* made her landfall off Boston, the skyscrapers and tower blocks rearing slowly above the olive-green coastline, Jason watched a group of men gathering in the well deck below the wheelhouse. At their head were Sails and Chippy, while behind them were Tregannon and Shiner Wright quietly mustering most of the crew. They stood sheepishly, looking furtively towards the wheelhouse where their Captain was leaning in his shirtsleeves through the bridge window. The remains of the shattered seaboat had been secured and the ship squared off.

There was a shout from Sails. They began singing, a raucous, unmelodious choir, but there was no mistaking its message. The Mate, Karl Karatz, was sick, confined to his cabin below. These men were mustered to tell their Captain, in their own fashion, that they respected his leadership and now stood loyally behind him. In the final count, intrigue had no place when men and their ship were fighting for survival. A lump rose in Mercer's gorge as he listened to the full-throated chorus of the age-old refrain. '*For he's a jolly good fellow…*'

Standing motionless at the bridge window, Captain Jones's cheeks coloured a shade and very slowly a smile drew across his face. In some way, Jason realized, *Windrose*'s company were bringing comfort to the man who had silently been mourning three of his men.

A distant tooting was heard from ahead: there was the Boston pilot boat and, not far off, the tug.

CHAPTER NINETEEN: HOME RUN

Jason Mercer would not forget in a hurry the reception which the people of Boston gave to the SACOR ships. These Bostonians were overwhelming with their hospitality: whoever you were, providing you were a participant in the great race, you were given the red-carpet treatment. It would have been good, he mused, to have shared it with Hannah.

Windrose, though her port boat was smashed, had suffered only superficial damage. And during those last six hours before Cape Cod, with his men behind him, Captain Barnaby Jones demanded, and received, an all-out effort from his crew. *Windrose* was scrubbed and polished from stem to stern; her sails and yards were trimmed; and even her sides were washed down to free her paintwork of salt after the battering she had suffered. Her enamel had been touched up, so that she shone like silver.

It was a marvellous moment, that early dawn of August the eleventh. Like so many Sundays in harbour, there was a stillness, a mirror-like calm on the surface of the blue sea, while the great barque glided on her engine towards Provincetown for the final hook of Cape Cod. At dawn, twenty miles to seaward, *Windrose* had been guided in by the beam from Nantucket, that beckoning haven after Helga's horrendous fury. The ship's crew was in the Ocean Shipping Line's uniform of traditional naval caps, white singlets and dark blue trousers; they were fallen in on deck while *Windrose* bore silently into Massachusetts Bay, past the whistle buoy and across Stellwagen Bank. Jason watched the impressive tower blocks, which dwarfed the older red-bricked buildings of Boston's original port, growing larger and larger.

With Flag 'G' flying at the peak of her spanker, the pilot boarded *Windrose* and took her up the north channel to the President Roads; past The Graves wrecks and into Number 17 Berth, where the container crane of Sea-Land Service was to prove such a boon. During the next six days, not only were repairs to be carried out, but it was obligatory for each SACOR competitor once again to hoist out ten container boxes and to embark twelve.

Only six days remained, that was all, before the variously battered ships had to be ready for the final 'off', on that next Sunday, 18 August. The Port Authorities, leaning backwards to help, courteously explained at the welcoming convention that their great port obviously could not risk groundings, either at the entrance or in the channel. Ships intending to start with the 1100 gun on that Sunday would have to sail on the Saturday and anchor overnight in Massachusetts Bay, outside the port limits. The start was a line on bearing 030° from the Highland lighthouse. Those next five days were unforgettable: miraculously, despite the frenetic hospitality, repairs to the damaged ships were completed.

For Captain Jones, his priority on arrival was a telephone call to the SACOR office to discover whether a message from Hannah was waiting for him: she *must* have been following the news of hurricane Helga. There was no cable, nothing.

He next telephoned his home in Warsash where she would be staying in England: no reply. So he rang *Wandering Star*. 'Fourth Officer Jones,' the guarded voice of the duty officer announced curtly, 'is ill and unfit for duty. She is confined to her bunk.' Upon insisting that he should be put through to her, Barnaby was dismayed and annoyed by Hannah's offhand attitude: she was all right but tired. She insisted on working her passage back to the UK in *Wandering Star*.

Barnaby slowly replaced the receiver: Hannah's response had been out of character. As soon as he had dealt with the problems of *Windrose*'s repairs, Barnaby would go round to *Wandering Star* and demand to see his daughter.

The Wind Ship Company, who had retro-fitted *Sherrilee* at Norwell on the North River, had taken *Windrose* under their wing. The barque's boat was replaced, the davits taken out, heat-treated and refitted; the after securing-chain deck bolts rewelded; the smashed port gunwale ripped out and repaired. *Windrose* was fortunate compared with some of the other ships.

Sao Isabel, the Portuguese vertical turbine windmill ship, had been repaired and was luckier than her rival, *Techno Phanta*, the horizontal turbine and Stok's windmill entry. *Phanta* had been heard passing her MAYDAY when the hurricane had recurved, her Captain's last horrified call reporting that during the abnormal rolling the tips of his windmill blades were threshing the troughs. Only one MAYDAY: that was all that was heard from her. Still no trace, lost with all hands, as also *Pollux*, the German four-masted dynaship. Like her sisters, her complicated reefing gear had failed: she had had trouble with her rotating masts and plastic sails. No one had been able to climb aloft. *Reina de la Mar* had got through safely, but her passengers had seen enough of the sea for a lifetime.

It was three days after *Windrose*'s arrival in Boston that the survivors from *Rêve de l'Avenir* had been flown in by chopper, having been transferred from the coastguard cutter off Nantucket. Nine men, that was all; and only one officer, the First Mate, Emile Crozier, whom Jason had liked. Jason went to see him in Massachusetts General Hospital where, suffering from acute exposure, they were nursing him back to life.

Surprisingly, Emile had wanted to talk about the foundering of the huge catamaran.

Rêve de l'Avenir had been caught in the dangerous quadrant. Trying to run free of it, she had been headed when the hurricane recurved. One of her two main alternators had been flooded by a freak sea and gone off the board to leave insufficient power to operate the after battery of 'sails'. So she had been forced to run before the storm until, finally, one 'float' was swamped by the breaking crest of a mountainous sea. The other 'float' unbelievably was left suspended in mid-air. The colossal stress on the structure had broken the ship's back, and fractured the central platform in half. For twenty minutes one section had floated, then been overwhelmed to disappear without a trace. The half on which Emile had found himself (he had gone aft to help with the upper deck cargo) floated long enough for a couple of inflatables to be slid into the water before she sank to take the bridge personnel with her. The rafts had survived the maelstrom, but Emile had been in the water for hours, the inflatables having been overblown like autumn leaves, and capsized time and time again. The searching planes had sighted their last flare.

On Saturday afternoon, two hours before the tugs came alongside, *Windrose* was ready for sea. Barnaby Jones, with the goodwill of his crew behind him, had brought the law to bear in order to discharge the undesirable elements of his company: all Stok's bunch. It had been easy to recruit replacement volunteers from the youth of Boston; the barque was happier now and as efficient under the leadership of Tregannon and Wright as she had ever been. Posner had been sent packing with Karatz, Tregannon being rated up to Boatswain.

During that forenoon, Captain Jones made a rushed visit to *Wandering Star* to see his daughter. Hannah looked deathly pale. 'We've got a virulent bug on board,' the nurse announced from the foot of the bed. 'It's getting us all down.'

Barnaby wasted no time. 'I'll arrange your transfer to the airport, Han: first flight to Heathrow. Aunt Penny will meet you: she's longing to make a fuss of you.'

Hannah pressed his hand and looked at him fixedly for a few seconds, her eyes round and large. 'No, I want to stay on.' Closing her eyes, she went on, 'I'm so tired, Dad,' her voice trailing to a whisper.

Barnaby tried to jolt her into talking about her voyage, but she did not even remember receiving a message from him. The conversation became pointless and he did not know what to make of the nurse firmly ensconced at the end of the bunk. He gently kissed his daughter and left abruptly, without saying another word.

'Thank God,' Captain Jones muttered to himself on his way back to *Windrose*, 'that Jason Mercer is doing his final stint in *Wandering Star*.' It was a comfort to know that the young man was an ally and could protect his beloved daughter on this last leg of the race. Jason was the right sort, Barnaby thought, of that he had no doubt.

On the next day, the Sunday forenoon of 18 August, it seemed that every Bostonian was either on the waterfront or in his boat gilling about Massachusetts Bay. Tugs hooted, firefloats fanned their jets in salute, aircraft and helicopters buzzed overhead. And as Mercer watched in isolation on the poop deck of *Wandering Star*, he felt lonelier than at any moment during these past three months. Hannah, taking the air on the nurse's arm, did not recognize him; Randy Buckle ignored him, Burn Tinewood had deliberately snubbed him.

Only the Bucko, Joào Otaz, the Portuguese mate, showed any civility by taking Jason to his poky cabin, a diminutive tin box immediately above the propeller.

If this is the way they wish to play it, thought Jason, *that's no skin off my nose. I'll do my own thing.* Just as well, because he could keep an eye on Hannah without suspicion of collusion. Things *were* hotting up: the result of the SACOR placings, loading and unloading times included, came in ten minutes before the first of the controlled starts. Buckle had pinned up the list on the bulkhead. He grinned maliciously at Jason and jerked his head towards the results stuck on the port screen:

Boston placing 1: *Flettner,* **Flag:** *Dutch,* **Name:** Mina, **Cargo:** *chemical ores,* **Intended discharge port:** *Felixstowe*

Boston placing 2: *Wind ship,* **Flag:** *USA,* **Name:** Sherrilee, **Cargo:** *chemical ores,* **Intended discharge port:** *Felixstowe*

Boston placing 3: *Schooner,* **Flag:** *Liberia,* **Name:** Wandering Star, **Cargo:** *engineering parts,* **Intended discharge port:** *Southampton*

Boston placing 4: *Airborne sails and kites,* **Flag:** *USA,* **Name:** Yankee Flyer, **Cargo:** *wool,* **Intended discharge port:** *Falmouth*

Boston placing 5: *Barque,* **Flag:** *British,* **Name:** Windrose, **Cargo:** *wool,* **Intended discharge port:** *Felixstowe*

Boston placing 6: *Schooner,* **Flag:** *USA,* **Name:** Sea Falcon, **Cargo:** *silicon,* **Intended discharge port:** *Felixstowe*

Boston placing 7: *Wingsail,* **Flag:** *Nigeria,* **Name:** Niger, **Cargo:** *liquid gas,* **Intended discharge port:** *Falmouth*

Boston placing 8: *Flettner,* **Flag:** *France,* **Name:** Jacques Yves Cousteau, **Cargo:** *coconut oil,* **Intended discharge port:** *Felixstowe*

Boston placing 9: *Schooner,* **Flag:** *Australia,* **Name:** Storm Petrel, **Cargo:** *kiwi fruit,* **Intended discharge port:** *Falmouth*

Boston placing 10: *Dynaship & Wingsail,* **Flag:** *Costa Rica,* **Name:** Red Star, **Cargo:** *mineral ore,* **Intended discharge port:** *Southampton*

Boston placing 11: *Bermudan sails,* **Flag:** *Saudi Arabia,* **Name:** Hijaz, **Cargo:** *tinned lamp,* **Intended discharge port:** *London*

Boston placing 12: *Windmill,* **Flag:** *Portugal,* **Name:** Sao Isabel, **Cargo:** *chemicals,* **Intended discharge port:** *Southampton*

Boston placing 13: *Fan & kite,* **Flag:** *Italy,* **Name:** Stella Venus, **Cargo:** *cars,* **Intended discharge port:** *Southampton*

Boston placing 14: *Barque,* **Flag:** *Spain,* **Name:** Reina de la Mar, **Cargo:** *passenger,* **Intended discharge port:** *Portsmouth*

Boston placing 15: *Airborne sails and kites,* **Flag:** *Singapore,* **Name:** Ocean Kite, **Cargo:** *grain,* **Intended discharge port:** *Liverpool*

Boston placing16: *Barque,* **Flag:** *Poland,* **Name:** Wicher,

Cargo: phosphates, *Intended discharge port:* Rotterdam

Mercer was thoughtful. There were still two thousand, eight hundred and sixty-three miles before reaching the finishing line off South Foreland. Much could happen in the next ten days: the SACOR organizers had not placed the line across the Strait of Dover for nothing, the most constricted shipping channel in the world.

CHAPTER TWENTY: UP CHANNEL

For day after day, Jason hoped that Hannah would show up. Captain Jones had insisted that Mercer's surveillance must be discretion itself, so the RO could only read the daily sick list: *Assistant Navigating Officer H. Jones — off duty.*

And, because he was shunned by the ship's officers, he spent most of his time watching them, noting every nuance, listening to their conversations. They were an unpleasant lot, the prison-like atmosphere seeming to emanate from their unpredictable Captain: Randy Buckle was driven by an obsession with winning the SACOR prize and he hated any rival who might deprive him of it. In the end, Jason's best moments were the few minutes he enjoyed with the seamen. Life on board *Wandering Star* was lonely for him during that crossing of the Northern Atlantic. He was so close to the woman he wanted to see and to protect. And often he wondered whether he had exaggerated the danger she was in; and would she accept his interference, anyway? He was perturbed by the fact that, although he had known Hannah for years, her image never left him completely now.

Without putting himself down for a shake, Jason turned out at dawn on that Wednesday, 28 August. Depression after depression had followed in the wake of Helga and, after ten days of grey skies and half-gales, he was not going to miss his first glimpse of England. Only two ships of the race had been sighted during the Atlantic passage, the advanced Flettner, *Mina*, the Dutchman who had consistently done well; and the Frenchman, *Jacques-Yves Cousteau*, the next-generation Flettner which the French had named an '*éolienne* turbo-sail'.

Her four vertical cylinders were rotated across her own relative wind by small generators injecting an air stream. Once started, the system was self-generating, the revolving cylinders producing the forward thrust component. Watching this ship, with its twenty-metres-high 'turbo-sails', sweeping effortlessly along, was a thrill for Jason Mercer. Named after the great man who devoted his life in trying to save the oceans from death, this competitor represented real hope, because Cousteau had long been derided and ignored, as geniuses so often were. It was good to see the *Jacques-Yves Cousteau* finishing among the leaders.

Jason wondered where *Windrose* was now. Was she still among the first six? And how would she fare after the computer calculations had been processed? Crossing the radar bearing line between South Foreland and Cap Gris Nez was only part of the game: there still remained the race to the ports and the timing of the cargo discharge, a coefficient which was an important factor in the calculations of the final overall profit, the factor which could decide the winner of SACOR. True, first-over-the-line was the unofficial winner between the skippers, for were they not running their own sweepstake? But much depended on the unloading, as the ship owners realized: *Wicher* was even being ordered to Rotterdam, where the Europort's reputation for efficient port handling and reliable stevedorage reigned supreme.

There...! The blip of the Bishop Rock light was showing on the PPI, at seventeen miles bearing 079°, on the expected bearing: Jason went out to the port quarter to try to sight the notorious lighthouse which protected the Scillies. Tinewood had not sighted the group-flashing buoy separating the north-south lane, because he had taken *Wandering Star* well south to make certain of entering the traffic lane on the southern and correct side. By 1030, she was well clear of the Pol Bank race, the Rock then being west of north. Within a few hours, Jason might be able to sight the flat promontory of The Lizard. He slipped back into the wheelhouse to check on the ship's progress.

Crouched over the chart was Burn Tinewood.

'Mind if I look at the chart?' Jason pitched the request abruptly.

'If you're interested.'

'I'm the RO,' Jason snapped. 'Remember?'

Buckle was at the window, and staring ahead at the shipping trailing westwards in the northern lane of the separation zone. He turned the ship over to the Third Mate, Donald Ferguson, grunted and then left the bridge. The interminable slatting of the five mainsails was jangling everyone's nerves. *Wandering Star* was at her worst in a light following wind: this breeze was no good to her.

'Call me if there's no freshening by the time we reach The Start,' Buckle ordered grumpily. 'I'll have to use the engines, if we're to keep up with *Mina* and *Sherrilee*.'

At 1430 Jason picked up the mauve haze to the north, the flat, grey wedge of The Lizard. It was good to see it again, this tangible proof that he could soon act to free Hannah from this tense situation. To his chagrin, he was certain that *Wandering Star* would be among the leaders, if not the outright winner of the SACOR fortune. She *must* be well ahead, because she had taken the northern route to the Western Approaches, and had enjoyed a broad reach for much of the Atlantic passage.

Just before sunset, *Sherrilee* and *Mina* were sighted ahead and ships' names were passed. Then, during the last of twilight, the loom of Start Point showed to the north. With those nostalgic three flashes piercing the darkness every ten seconds, Jason felt relieved that *Wandering Star*, this Liberian ship, with its cosmopolitan crew and owned by the ruthless Stok, was at least inside British territorial waters. Buckle and his cronies were now answerable to British law for Hannah Jones's safety. Having noted that Tinewood had reported the ship's position at 2215, when passing the Channel light vessel, Jason turned in, bidding 'goodnight' only to Joào Otaz, who was taking over the midnight-to-four.

Jason could not sleep: the engines were pounding beneath him and the beat of the propellers was thumping perpetually in his ears. Finally, he went on deck to watch the dawn coming up and to take his readings. He did not want to miss the passage of the Dover Strait later, so he would make up his records early.

He stood by himself on the after deck, his face fanned by the light breeze. He shivered and drew the collar of his jacket closer about his neck. It was 0415 and to the east the dawn clouds were already flushed the rose-pink of the inside of a coral shell. Streaks of duck-egg green flaked the dispersing cirrus, while to the westward the indigo clouds of night were packing up to disperse like sulking children, range after range of them, as the sun's warmth invaded the late August dawn. But to the north, low and hiding the downs of England from sight, an ominous bank of cold, grey cotton-wool was rapidly building up. Fog was about: he could feel its clammy, cold fingers in the air.

It was Thursday, 29 August, the day when *Wandering Star* and perhaps others would be crossing the finishing line. How many miles off was it now? Jason stepped into the wheelhouse to squint again at the chart. The five o'clock DR put her due south of Selsey and abreast the halfway mark of Seine Bay. He would get cleaned up, then come up for another look before breakfast. It was maddening having to cross the line and then having to double back. Presumably Stok knew what he was doing and had already fixed the Southampton container port: his dockies would have every inducement to discharge in record time...

'*Sail. Right aft, sir. Just above the horizon.*'

There was a rush for the doors. Jason left through the leeward side and heard Otaz muttering, 'That's *Windrose*. God Almighty! Look, Mr Mercer.' He handed over his binoculars. 'Look how she's going, Mister...'

It was all that Jason could do not to whistle. His circle of vision focused on a tiny speck which, even as he watched, enlarged to become distinguishable: the fore royal of a fully-rigged ship, most probably. Handing back the glasses, Jason went below to fetch his own binoculars. By the time he returned, Buckle was on the bridge: the distant royal had been augmented by a fore upper topgallant. Then came the head of an outer jib. The overtaking ship could only be *Windrose*, with those tall masts of the same height.

An half an hour later, the identification was confirmed: *Windrose* under full sail, with every stitch of canvas she could carry, was overhauling swiftly from the westward. With this perfect following wind she was gaining at three knots and, unless the wind either died or blew hard, *Wandering Star* could do nothing about it. Buckle summoned both watches and for over an hour tinkered with the sheets. But nothing he could do prevented the maddening slatting of the five mainsails which were blanketing the headsails. And if he tacked downwind, he would be adding too many unnecessary miles. As the forenoon wore on, food and rest were ignored while the tension built up, the great barque gaining relentlessly with every half-hour.

At nine o'clock, Beachy was due north: Royal Sovereign passed to the west; and then at 1145, *Wandering Star* altered further to the southward to 041° off the Bassurelle lightship for the final run up to the finishing line. *Windrose* was, by Tinewood's radar range, only four miles astern. Buckle was aiming to approach the French coast as close as he dared: after crossing the finishing line between Gris Nez and South Foreland, *Wandering Star* needed the best possible wind slant for Spithead and the Southampton container terminal. *Windrose* was overtaking at three knots, but Buckle's expletives were failing to extract one extra revolution from the *Star*'s engines which were now pounding away.

CHAPTER TWENTY-ONE: THE STRAIT

Captain Buckle stood astride, hands in his trouser pockets and glaring at the great barque sweeping up from astern. He hated that ship and loathed her Master's guts as much as he admired *Windrose*'s resplendent power and grace. She lived up to her name: a rose of the winds and the ocean in full summer bloom.

Officers and crew emerged from below to watch the splendid ship thunder past: even the nurse, Jasmine Htut, had come up, bringing her sick charge with her. And once again, Buckle recognized that rage erupting deep inside him, a pulsing throb in his eardrums, his chest heaving, a rising tension fast reaching the danger level...

Merely a glimpse of that girl, that sickly, pale daughter of Jones's, was more than enough for him at the moment. The Assistant Navigating Officer had been kept sedated to render her docile ... but, though still a useful pawn in the game, she was a damned nuisance. In Buckle's field of vision there were *Windrose* and Hannah, and both were intolerable.

'God!' Tinewood blurted at Buckle's elbow. 'Just look at her, how she's going!' Standing on the deck of the floundering schooner whose sails slatted in the wind as she pumped along under engines, Captain Buckle sensed that somehow his men, mesmerized by *Windrose*'s performance, were virtually deserting him. If *Wandering Star* was not hemmed in by the separation zones and the IMCO rules for the Strait, he would have tacked downwind on broad reaches and been able to challenge *Windrose*.

The anger simmering inside Buckle was building up to explosion point. His compulsion to dominate had been the cause of deep rifts between his family and himself, as well as between his friends. He remained a mercenary to his pride, for how otherwise would he have used every artifice to seduce his brother's girlfriend? She had not resisted for long the excitement which the chase had given them. But the punishment had been as violent as the conquest, which had brought him little pleasure: his victory had been followed by a wave of remorse and a sense of total isolation. And the cycle continued to recur whenever a challenge presented itself. Despair was never far from the surface to counter-balance his bullying and bluster, which were all part of his act, of that he was well aware: this was the Randy Buckle image, the flaming beard, the rumbustious, rollicking humour. But he could never forget his brother calling him a 'schizo', another factor which had turned him into a loner. Winning had been an obsession all his life: he *had* to win this SACOR. *That* would show them, and the fortune would alter the direction of his life.

With all sails billowing, every stitch of canvas set and drawing perfectly, a bone flashing at her stem, *Windrose* was already easing to starboard to clear the schooner by less than a cable when she romped past.

What the hell was Jones up to now? Godammit, he was cutting *inside* the schooner! *Windrose* was steering between *Wandering Star*'s stern and the shallows to the north of The Ridge shingle bank, a nasty patch with less than two metres over it at low water. Buckle glanced at his watch: less than an hour to low water — and today was 'springs', with the tides at their worst. Jones was staking his all on this crazy decision, and for a secret instant Captain Buckle longed to see that vast billowing cloud of canvas crashing to a cataclysmic halt, the sticks toppling out of the barque as she charged aground on the bank...

'For God's sake!' Buckle bellowed blasphemously. 'Hard a-port!'

He could hear the seas swirling under *Windrose*'s bilge keels as she plunged onwards, the south-westerly wind bearing her ahead at a good twenty knots. Then her forefoot, plunging downwards in the yellowy-green seas poppling across The Ridge, reared upwards to shoot a cloud of spindrift flying the length of her. If Jones was lucky enough to clear the patch, for sure *Windrose* would be caught on the Varne, that treacherous bank close northward of The Ridge.

The two ships were less than two cables apart when *Wandering Star* began swinging to port. Buckle could see Jones clearly now, waving from *Windrose*'s poop deck. There was something in that cocky way he stood astride, his condescending greeting which drove the Master of the *Star* to blind fury. His glance darted to the gleeful RO, Mercer, then switched to his grinning officers; and there was that girl, Hannah Jones, standing there, deathly pale, not understanding what was going on.

'Nothing's barred,' Buckle's boss, Akroyd Stok, had confided. 'Nothing, d'ye hear, Captain Buckle, so long as *Wandering Star* wins SACOR?' And when Stok had realized that *Windrose* was a prospective rival, he had not hesitated an instant to use the girl as hostage to fortune...

Hostage to fortune... A fiery, crimson mist floated before the crazed Master's gaze. A mad glint in his wild eyes, he barged towards his female navigator. Grabbing her, he pushed her to the stern. Then, before anyone could move, he swivelled the girl over the rail and hove her over the stern.

There was a second's stunned silence while they watched the frail girl flailing in the threshing wake. Then, while Ferguson, the Third Mate, leapt for the lifebuoy, Jason tore off his jacket and sprang to the rail. Otaz grappled with his crazed skipper. Tinewood, hesitating a second, yelled at the helmsman to reverse the wheel before he, too, flung himself upon the frenzied Master. Jason, balancing an instant upon the rail, shoved with his legs and plunged into the sea.

The shock of hitting the water knocked the wind from Jason's lungs, but jerked him to reality: Hannah had no lifejacket, was a drugged woman and was already more than a hundred yards distant. His arms flailed as he swam with a frenzied crawl towards that dark head bobbing elusively in the water.

Jason had but one compelling drive: he must get to Hannah. *Dear God, keep her afloat long enough...* Gasping for breath as he swallowed the salty water, he desperately closed the distance. His whole frame ached with the intense effort, his muscles burning, beginning to fail. As his strokes became weaker and weaker, he prayed to his God as never before. His body continued blindly to obey the programmed orders from his brain, but now he could hardly reach forward for his next swimming stroke... Then he saw the gleam of a glistening orange lifebuoy, its calcium flare spluttering with browny-orange smoke. He dragged from himself a final spurt and fell across the buoy, his lungs bursting. And as he slipped into the horseshoe, he searched around him: *there* she was, *there* — in the short seas, barely ten yards away.

Hannah!

He swam breaststroke the final gap of water. Her frightened eyes fastened on his. Pushing the buoy before him and threshing with his legs, the last few yards seemed an eternity.

But, at last, her hand clamped on the far side of the horseshoe. He swivelled the buoy round, dog-paddled beside her and thrust her into its opening while he kept his left hand on the line. When, momentarily, he plunged below the surface, he heard the 'singing' of a boat's propeller. Shaking his head when he came up for air, he heard the blissful clattering of a fast-running diesel. A motor cutter was lurching down upon them and, in the bows, he saw the friendly face of Leading Seaman Tregannon shouting at him. A heaving-line plopped across Jason's face and seconds later *Windrose*'s boat plucked them both from the sea.

They laid Hannah in the sternsheets. Her cheeks were already purple, her mouth blue when Tregannon wrapped her in the blanket. Jason choked on the fiery rum which a seaman was trickling between his trembling lips. Then Sails yanked over the tiller and steered back to the barque who was hove-to, her topsails backed, her bell clanging in the clammy wisps of yellow-green fog beginning to swirl about the ship. As the boat was hoisted from the lop, Jason Mercer heard the baleful blare of a fog diaphone blasting close to starboard.

'The Varne,' Sails said. 'The Old Man will soon have us home.' Then he added grimly, 'And he'll be having Buckle's guts for garters.'

CHAPTER TWENTY-TWO: SHIFTING SANDS

Of *Wandering Star* there was no sign when they finally heaved Jason to his feet. He stood in his own pools of water upon *Windrose*'s deck, gasping for air when Captain Jones came towards him.

'Thanks, Jason. Hannah will be all right,' the Master said quietly. 'She's bringing up all that she's swallowed. We'll keep her in sick bay.'

The Master's eyes were everywhere, checking the sails as they brought the great ship again before the wind. Never had Jason respected *Windrose*'s Captain so much as at this moment: deprived of a chance of winning SACOR's gigantic prize by the despicable action of his closest rival, Jones remained under complete self-control, hands behind his back, his solid figure turned towards the welldeck. Then, as he watched the hands moving with accustomed agility to man the braces, something seemed to be unleashed within him.

Reaching for his loud-hailer, he barked down the length of the upper deck. 'By God!' he bellowed. '*Wandering Star*'s not won yet. Come on, men, give the ship all you've got!' And as they walked Jason unsteadily below for a warm shower, the cheers of *Windrose*'s company rang and re-echoed in his ears. The crew's dander was up, too, by the sound of it.

Down below, while he dressed, Jason heard, every half minute, the mournful dirge from the diaphone of the Varne lightship blasting close to port. He returned on deck which, to his surprise, was again bathed in a pale sunlight; the ship was on port tack, and dancing across the sparkling sea for the Folkestone shore which was in sight already through the misty glare.

'Better?' Barnaby Jones enquired, lowering his binoculars. Uncharacteristically, he wrung the RO's hand. 'Thanks, Jason,' he repeated. 'The end of a nightmare.'

Jason's embarrassment was averted by the appearance of Frank Sisson, the Radio Officer. 'An interesting signal just in from Felixstowe Dock, sir. They've got a vacant berth to offer: first-come, first-served.'

The Master squinted at the message which was held before him. He looked up. 'No trouble with our arrival signal?'

'No, Captain. I passed it through Land's End Radio, and it was acknowledged by Harwich. Berth D3 has just been confirmed. No container cranes.'

'Damn… We'll have to use our gear, then.' The Master looked across at Bellew. 'All right, First?'

The Mate nodded. 'I'll get the gear ready, sir.'

'It'll be interesting to see what Buckle does with Felixstowe's offer,' Jones remarked. 'Can you monitor Harwich Radio, Sparks?'

'Yes, Captain. The *Star*'s booked for Southampton.' Frank Sisson returned to his radio room.

The Master was staring into the radar, his face concealed by the visor. 'I've found *Wandering Star*,' he told Tudgey, who was now acting as navigating officer. 'Keep track of her.' Jones handed over the PPI and stared through his binoculars to the east of the white and red jumble which was Folkestone. 'There's the pilot boat,' he announced to Jason. He lowered his glasses. 'I'm picking up Jack Kilner in Eastwear Bay. He's an old chum and the best Trinity House pilot in the business. I rang him yesterday off The Lizard. He'll take us up to the Sunk.'

This lightship was off Harwich and it was here that the Felixstowe pilots boarded. True to his profession, Jones was taking no risks, even in this vital SACOR challenge, thought Jason. He was certainly a prudent mariner. Once again, he admired the skill with which Jones handled his great sailing ship as the main and mizzen yards were backed to pick up the pilot. The ladder was unrolled and hung over the side; the black and buff launch plunged alongside, its red and white flag flapping loudly in the breeze. Spray shot upwards, the pilot leaped for the rungs of the ladder and then the boat was sheering off, another job accomplished. Barnaby stood at the rail to meet his old friend. A seaman took Captain Kilner's steaming-bag and, as soon as greetings were exchanged, the yards were squared and she was running again up channel, the wind fresh but, sensed Jason, beginning to moderate. *Windrose* was now on the starboard tack and going well in the inshore lane.

It seemed to Jason only minutes before the austere outline of Dover castle was glaring down at them only two miles off. It was now 1415 on this 29 August; the tide was flooding, and the ship was bowling along at twenty-two knots for the South Goodwin light vessel, her heading 069°. He shivered while he stood on *Windrose*'s poop and stared at those white cliffs. The tall radio masts slipped past; the conspicuous clock tower faded; and the surveillance station perched on the cliff edge of St Margaret's Bay, just north of the massive headland of South Foreland, came abeam of them and then passed astern. The Dover Patrol Memorial hove in sight as Jason again felt the clammy cold. Ahead he heard two diaphone blasts reverberating and, turning to starboard, he saw a bank of oily, green fog curling around the South Goodwin lightship. In seconds, the vessel had been blotted out. And as he stepped into the wheelhouse for warmth, Sparks hurried in with a signal for the Master.

'I've picked up *Wandering Star* talking through North Foreland Radio,' he reported. 'She's having a go for the vacant berth at Felixstowe.'

'Where is she now?' Jones rapped at Tudgey. 'Hurry up, man.'

Tiny Tudgey was already bent over the PPI and adjusting the brilliance and the bearing strobe. '2930, sir.' He twiddled the range knob. 'Four point two miles.' He paused, then added, 'There's something wrong with the set, sir. I'm getting poor definition.'

Windrose's Master was standing apart from the others, staring into the thick fog swirling down upon them. For an instant he remained silent. Then he turned to the pilot. 'Take me up the South Falls passage, please, Jack. I'm taking the canvas off her. Start the siren, Mister.'

He strode to the engine console, talked on the phone to the Chief. A minute later the engine rumbled into life, the ship trembled. A prolonged blast shattered the peace.

Windrose was entering the busiest and most constricted channel in the world: already Jason could hear the whistle buoy fine on the starboard bow, the buoy marking the dividing line between the main traffic lane and the inshore route inside the South Falls.

'Captain…' Tudgey called from his radar visor. 'The *Star*'s in the Downs. Looks as if she's taking the Gull Stream channel, inside the Goodwins.'

'Where is she?'

'Off Deal Bank and heading into the Gull Stream off Ramsgate.'

'She's an hour ahead already, then,' Jones snapped. 'But I'm not increasing my revolutions, Jack, in spite of her lead. This fog is too thick, when I've a duff radar.' He shouted across the deck to his Mate, 'Have both anchors ready for letting go, Mister.'

'Aye, aye, sir.'

'Steer 0500,' the Pilot commanded. 'Alter course to 360° when the Horn buoy comes abeam in ten minutes' time.'

And as the siren blared again, once every two minutes, Jason felt thankful he was sailing under a prudent captain. The race was on now. But Extra Master Jones was not going to hazard his ship, whatever risks his rival was prepared to take.

On board *Wandering Star*, after a brief battle of wills, Otaz, the First Mate, reluctantly handed command of the schooner back to her appointed master. Joào Otaz was convinced that his Captain was mentally deranged. After the man's frenzied rage and its criminal result of throwing Hannah Jones overboard, the Portuguese Mate's opinion was confirmed by Buckle's latest action. The schooner's officers could do nothing about the situation, unless there was a concerted 'Caine Mutiny' effort. Things had happened too quickly, Joào realized. '*Caldera de Pedro Botello*!' he swore to himself. Hell! An hour since the emergency. And two minutes ago, Captain Buckle, having refused to take a pilot, made the spontaneous decision to go flat out for the vacant berth at Felixstowe. It had required all Burn Tinewood's persuasion to stop Buckle from cancelling the *Star*'s reserved berth in the Southampton Container Terminal.

Madness seemed to have a firm grip of the Master now. Despite the deteriorating visibility and the forecast of fog, Buckle had taken the *Star* across the lanes at a narrow angle, so acute that St Margaret's Bay must be watching and reporting her to the authorities. 'God help us,' Joào muttered, and he began to stroll forward to see that the for'd lookouts were in place and alert.

The fog was thick now, but Buckle was still leaving his canvas hoisted. 'Wind's gonna shift,' he announced with a slur to his voice.

Back aft in the wheelhouse, the Bo'sun's Mate was sounding the siren every two minutes, a racket which always jangled Tinewood's nerves. But this afternoon he barely noticed it: he seemed to be living in an *Alice in Wonderland* world where all the rules were being turned topsy-turvy. He had difficulty in persuading Buckle even to prepare an anchor for letting go. He shrugged his shoulders and dived again into the radar. He'd con the ship himself if he could only persuade the lunatic skipper to leave the bridge... He twiddled the controls for a decent picture on the PPI, just as the Brake bell buoy showed on the close-range scale. He told the Quartermaster to steer ten degrees to starboard, for safety's sake in this restricted channel.

Tinewood had been into The Downs only once in his life, when his Captain had anchored during this sort of vile fog: oily, green stuff, swirling about the masts and so thick that he could not see even the forestay and bowsprit. He had never been up the Gull Stream, and this initiation was making his flesh creep. He wished that he had the ROFAC guides to help him: there was too much bumph to assimilate. The shipping fraternity owed much to Dickie Richardson, who had pioneered these aids to navigation and who had devoted his life to bringing order out of chaos in the shipping lanes.

Buckle had bellowed when Tinewood had eased the revolutions. The maniac had immediately gone straight up to three-quarter speed and, with the spring flood under her, *Wandering Star*'s log was showing thirteen knots, *thirteen knots!* And, with her canvas still hoisted, not a chance in hell of stopping in an emergency. His face hidden inside the visor of the radar, Tinewood shook his head in despair. The baleful clanging of the port-hand buoy passed swiftly down the port side, and Tinewood just had time to dash on to the wings to identify it positively: Thank God! Red can, its name *Brake...* Now for the NW and North Goodwin buoys, the tricky bit, where the shallow patches were. With her 5.9 metres draught, *Wandering Star* should scrape safely over them ... and then, peering into the PPI again, he saw a fresh blip right ahead, just smudging the two-mile ring.

The screen was displaying well, the drying patches of sand of the Goodwins showing distinctly a couple of miles abeam to starboard. Even the wrecks stood out starkly (in the Ramsgate pubs they still called it The Graveyard, a grim reminder of the wartime convoys and shelling); there was Goodwin Knoll, North Sand Head and, a mile to the north, the North Goodwin Light Vessel. God! After all the drama of the past couple of hours, he'd be relieved to be safely through the Gull Stream and past Broadstairs Knoll... And Tinewood longed to know whether Hannah Jones was safe, and the RO all right: he *must* presume so, because surely *Windrose* would have come up on the radio, with help from Dover and Folkestone so close?

'North West Goodwin starboard hand bell buoy one cable,' he reported to his crazy Captain. 'Fine, starboard bow.'

Buckle grunted, continued to stare for'd where the five mainsails slatted uselessly. It was like being in a spaceship adrift in the limitless universe. Nothing, save the whorls of swirling fog ... and then Tinewood thought he could hear the clanging of a bell, very faint, a tinny noise from the direction of the North Goodwin buoy. He stuck his head back into the radar: nothing, just the advancing, southbound ship now seven hundred yards off and passing down the port side, nice and safe. Twice he had heard her siren; her blasts were becoming more imperious with each two-minute interval...

'She's passing to port, Captain,' Tinewood called out. 'Six hundred yards, large echo.' Why, for Pete's sake, did not Buckle stop his engines, behave rationally? They were all in a Catch 22 trap, unable to act, save mutinously. Burn Tinewood tried to comfort himself by acknowledging that at least the appalling risks which Buckle was taking, his crass and criminal behaviour, could win the race. And once the money was in Tinewood's pocket, riches would swiftly dull any feeling of guilt which he might harbour.

The shadowy outline of the North West Goodwin buoy swished down the starboard side. The black buoy and its topmark juddered in the swirl of the tidal stream; its bell clanged, weirdly, sadly. Then suddenly it was gone, bubbling and hissing astern. North Goodwin starboard-hand next, then the Gull Stream before the last two buoys which formed the northern gate into the inshore channel, the Gull and Goodwin Knoll. Thank God! Almost there... He submerged himself into the radar again, the fluorescent PPI and its steadily revolving strobe giving him the only sense of security he had felt for a long time. He switched over to the long-range scale, just in case.

The new picture was reassuring, ships being concentrated entirely in the main shipping lanes, well east of the Goodwins. There was only one vessel in the South Falls and her echo could well be *Windrose*'s: 14,000 yards, 1150 and just north of the South Falls buoy. If that *was* her, the *Star* would be well ahead at the Sunk lightship, even if the falling wind held as it was, and she continued under power. With a feeling of satisfaction, Tinewood switched back to close-range.

'What will be my course for the Sunk, Second?' Buckle shouted his question, his voice abrasive in the quiet wheelhouse. 'Do I have to clear the Elbow before I can set my new heading?'

Tinewood remained peering at his PPI. 'Ship at two cables, Captain.' His bearing and distance report was drowned by the invisible vessel's whistle, at the end of which Tinewood thought he heard a shout on the wind from for'd.

'D'ye hear me, Mr Tinewood? I'm waiting for a course to the Sunk and Felixstowe, damn you.'

Tinewood stomped angrily over to the chart table; he was at the limit of his self-control. Couldn't this maniac contain his impatience a few minutes longer, until this hazardous passage was completed? To hell with Buckle! He angrily rolled his parallel ruler across the chart, making it shriek.

While he was marking off the course line, the approaching ship's siren blasted from the port bow: North Goodwin buoy next and very soon, right ahead... There was a cry from for'd, then a shout, he was sure, from one of the lookouts, in the eyes of the ship.

'What's the idiot want?' Buckle snapped at Joào Otaz. 'Why doesn't he use the phone?'

The question was never answered, for as Tinewood emerged from the chart table to check upon the development, he heard a ship's bell ringing from ahead, very close.

'There's a bell ringing ahead, sir.' It was the lookout shouting, his hands waving frenziedly towards the bow. 'Saw her through a gap in the fog, sir. *She's anchored...*'

At that instant, to the frantic bell-ringing were added French voices yelling in the fog from ahead. Without waiting for orders, Tinewood shoved the Quartermaster from the wheel and swung the telegraphs to 'emergency astern'. As the schooner trembled the length of her, a shadowy outline showed fine on the *port* bow in the dispersing, yellowy fog. There was nothing that Tinewood could do, but to slam the wheel over to starboard: the southbound ship was passing down the port side, less than two cables off. Dead ahead was the anchored French trawler.

It seemed an eternity, an eternity during which the schooner's knife-like bows refused to swing, her shadowy bowsprit aimed like a spear at the enlarging silhouette of the trawler. Tinewood braced himself for the collision, waited for the shock...

Slowly the schooner's bow began to pay off, then started to swing rapidly to starboard. The trawler, a black, identifiable outline now, slid down the *Star*'s side, her stern gantry catching the Thursday mast's boom-end. There was a ripping, tearing sound, the screaming of tortured metal when the schooner's port quarter caught the trawler's bow and anchor cable...

Then both ships sprang apart. *Wandering Star*'s bows reared suddenly into the air. Losing way, she grated slowly to a halt, as Tinewood flung himself at the console and threw the telegraphs to 'stop'.

'Goodwin Knoll,' he swore to himself. 'There're only three patches and we've had to find one of 'em...'

CHAPTER TWENTY-THREE:
'...WHERE WE WOULD BE.'

It was so quiet on the bridge of *Windrose* that Jason could still hear the horn of the South Falls buoy sounding off on the barque's starboard quarter. Jack Kilner, the pilot, stood immobile alongside his lifelong friend, the Master of *Windrose*, as both listened intently in the eerie silence. Across the Sands to the westward, they could pick up the sound of a ship's bell ringing faintly and, from the same direction, the three distant blasts from the North Goodwin lightship.

'It could be lifting,' Captain Jones muttered. 'What d'you think, Jack?'

The pilot shook his head, rubbed his eyes. 'I'm beginning to see things where there ain't nothing,' he laughed. 'There's hope, though: the wind's freshening again.'

Wrapped in his thick sweater, Jason Mercer stood next to the two seafarers. He was feeling warmer, but it had taken all this time since his immersion, nearly an hour and a half, for his circulation to start pumping again. He felt his strength returning. The realization that Hannah was safe and sound prompted his recovery. He was happy and hopeful.

'If vis. improves, will you set sail again for Felixstowe?' Kilner asked. 'The wind's steady, but...'

'PAN-PAN-PAN,' the loudspeaker on the after bulkhead suddenly crackled, 'PAN-PAN-PAN.' The voice seemed familiar to Jason. 'This is auxiliary schooner *Wandering Star*, *Wandering Star*, *Wandering Star*...'

The bridge personnel froze where they stood. *Windrose*'s siren blared defiantly, and then the *Star*'s distress signal was being repeated: 'Position: Goodwin Knoll. Collision with fishing-boat. I am aground.'

Seconds later, came the rapid MAYDAY from the French ship saying that she was making water and could be sinking. North Foreland was on the air within seconds. The steady voice of the coastguard lent its calm authority, as he took charge.

'She's only two and a half miles from us, sir,' Tudgey said from his chart table. 'Inside the Knoll.'

Jones had put on port wheel and the barque was already easing to port.

'Stay on course, Captain,' the pilot advised. 'At the moment, you're on the correct side of the channel. You can't do anything to help, with your draught. They'll soon have that idiot off the Sands, with the flood under her.'

Jason observed the two seamen: between them they shared over sixty years of experience, and if they could have helped they would have been the first. There was little danger of loss of life and, anyway, the busiest port in the world with its back-up and lifeboat was within only half an hour…

'Course 014° for Felixstowe and the Sunk light vessel, sir,' Tudgey called out, putting away his ROFAC for the Brest-Elbe area. These guides made a navigator's existence bearable, in the way they condensed things.

While *Windrose* settled to her course, they listened to Buckle slowly sorting himself out. The *Star* was in no danger and would probably come off, nearer high water. The aggrieved trawler was limping back to Boulogne and no one was hurt. The wind freshened and blew away the fog. Jones set sail and soon the barque was clipping along again at nineteen knots.

When the sun finally burnt through, Jason watched the Thames shipping plying in and out of the estuary, while the great ship rolled onwards to her final destination.

The Tongue drifted by, they left Kentish Knock to port at 1620 and, at 1645, altered course to 305°. Kilner did not know the local pilot whom they took on board at 1710 off the Sunk lightship; he was picked up in record time so that they could be at Felixstowe docks before they shut down for the night. The Ship wash bank slid past and then, at 1745, hands were called to get the sail off her and to prepare for entering harbour. To the cheers of the small watching crowd, the barque, sails furled and under the control of two tugs, was being nudged alongside D3 berth in the vast, modern port of Felixstowe. She had made it by three minutes: at six o'clock the whistles began blowing.

'Just in time, Cap'n,' the grizzled Felixstowe pilot told Barnaby as he left the ship with Captain Kilner. 'We wanted you alongside before they shut down for the night.'

By 1900, *Windrose* was secured on D3 Berth. The hands went to supper, the Bo'sun asking that they should rig the derricks and unloading gear as soon as they had eaten. Gavin McBinney came on board with Felixstowe's harbour master. Barnaby Jones asked Jason to join him at his table, where McBinney brought his partner up to date with events. It was a happy reunion, and afterwards they retired to the wheelhouse. From there, the Master could watch the unloading.

Jones was not losing a second, because the race was not ended until the last container box was on the quayside. The first question Barnaby had asked was who had arrived before him at Felixstowe. Sharing the list with the others, Jason was surprised to note how well the aerofoils and Flettners had done: *Sherrilee* and *Niger* were in, and so was *Jacques-Yves*

Cousteau. Sea Falcon was due during the early hours and *Reina de la Mar*, the Spanish passenger ship designed by Colin Mudie, tomorrow night. *Mina*, the Dutch Flettner, was in the English Channel and should be at Europort tomorrow, followed closely by the Pole, *Wicher*. The others had not yet crossed the line nor entered the channel, and most of the big boys would be unloading at other ports.

'What are our chances, Gavin?' Barnaby asked, a twitch at the corner of his mouth. 'Silly question, at this stage...'

McBinney was serious when he said shortly, 'I reckon we're well in the running. We've done well so far, but we're sunk if we don't win. Let's get on with it and unload this stuff.' He stripped off his jacket, flung it in the corner and rolled up his shirt sleeves. The door slid back and a man in an open-necked shirt and well-worn jeans entered.

'Jim Doggart,' he introduced himself. 'Shop steward.'

Through the windows, Jason could see the hands bustling along the upper deck, dragging booms, derricks and tackles after them. There was an air of urgency about all they did: the First Mate was standing amidships to supervise the double-staying of the masts with the pneumatic presses which had been especially designed for just this evolution. There was a whimsical twinkle in Doggart's eyes when Barnaby asked, 'What about the unions, Mr Doggart? Do they accept my men unloading?'

'"Jim" to my mates, Cap'n,' the stevedore's representative growled. 'Nae bother, Cap'n. Management and unions run this private port together, like a ship.' He went on in his soft Edinburgh accent, 'Makes sense, don't it? Och, I've plenty of volunteers to gi' ye a hand, if ye rig the gear.'

And so, while Jason helped *Windrose*'s RO to fill up the log entries, the barque was prepared for discharging her cargo. The handling drills upon which Captain Jones had insisted so often, while other ships were enjoying their runs ashore, were now paying off. The temporary forestay and the four triatic stays were set up; then the five lower stays were released by the hydraulic releasing gear. 'Chippy' Hicks, the carpenter, was everywhere, overseeing the running rigging to avoid it fouling the jibs of the ship's cranes. As soon as the yards were cock-billed to avoid damage, the crane operators, who were the ship's own engineers, began to plumb the nineteen-metre jibs over the container boxes and hatches. The automatic cut-outs on the slewing motors prevented the jibs from being swung too low or beyond the safe training area.

Jason was impressed by the ease and quiet efficiency with which it all worked. He was able to time the operation, box by box, able to watch the slick unloading. The mast carried the topping-lifts, the heels of which were fitted to slewing rings encircling the masts. Manipulating their machinery to handheld control buttons, the crane drivers could watch every movement under the arc-lights which had been rigged.

The final box was landed on the quayside as the dawn broke blood-red above *Sherrilee*'s funnel in the next dock. The MacGregor hatches were lowered back in place, the jibs housed on the hatch covers; and then the topping-lifts were lowered down to the heel, so that once more the courses could be set. And when the last operator shouted his final report, *Windrose*'s RO pushed his stop-watch button for the last time. For *Windrose*, SACOR was at an end.

Jason Mercer turned to watch the staunch Master whose courage had brought this ship and her crew home safely. After all they had been through together, Jason felt very close to the Joneses. Father and daughter needed a rest, after their ordeals. This SACOR had been quite a race.

Stok's *Wandering Star* could still win, if she got off the Goodwins smartly: she could still be at Southampton by this afternoon's tide, still be *Windrose*'s closest rival. Though the barque had been pipped across the line by the criminal action of *Wandering Star*'s crazy skipper, Captain Jones deserved more than respect.

And as for Hannah, Jason wondered, however tough she appeared to be, would she accept him caring for her? He smiled wistfully. And as he moved slowly towards the companionway leading below, the tired and unshaven stevedore leader approached.

'Ye might like to know,' he said, nodding his shaggy head, 'that the Southampton dockies aren't unloading yet. They're striking, demanding more money for this SACOR job.' He was grinning all over his blue-jowled face. 'Perhaps ye'll tell the Old Man, will ye, sir?'

A NOTE TO THE READER

Dear Reader,
If you have enjoyed the novel enough to leave a review on **Amazon** and **Goodreads**, then we would be truly grateful.

Sapere Books is an exciting new publisher of brilliant fiction and popular history.

To find out more about our latest releases and our monthly bargain books visit our website:
saperebooks.com